Love Lied

The Love Series

Book #1

By:

Keta Kendric

Keta Kendric/Hot Pen Publishing, LLC
P.O. Box 55060
Virginia Beach, VA 23471

Cover by: Author King Ellie

Edited by: A. L. Barron

ISBN: 978-1-956650-17-4/Love Lied

Contents

Synopsis:

Charlene: The decimation of my ten-year relationship destroyed me, crushed my soul into a heap of dust. Time healed the bulk of my brokenness, but I refused to relinquish myself to another…until Ransome came dancing his way into my life. Wickedly sexy, all I needed was one night with him to douse my desires.

Ransome: My job as a dancer didn't inspire relationship hopes in the minds of any self-respecting woman. I wanted more, but drunken nights of sex and one-night stands summarized my unflattering relationship status. Finding a woman willing to give me a chance was as unattainable as picking winning lottery numbers…until my eyes gleamed into the darkness and found Charlene.

Warning: This is a multicultural contemporary romance that contains explicit sexual content and is intended for adults.

Chapter One

Charla

A blubbering mess.

This is what I had become, a blob of emotional wreckage edging toward depression. I never expected to end up alone after spending a decade in a relationship I assumed would be everlasting.

The strong foundation the relationship was built on was no more than a fallacy I tricked myself into believing was real. Now, I'm here, lost in my own misery.

Single was a disease I assumed I was too good to catch. Timothy Carter, the man I dedicated years of my life to, didn't want me anymore. He packed a bag one night and left me for another woman. His swift actions were out of the blue and so erratic that the impact was a devastating blow I didn't see coming.

My female intuition told me years ago that something was amiss, but I didn't want to acknowledge it. I didn't want to accept that I didn't do enough to keep my man from straying or enough to keep him from leaving me.

I should have accepted that Carter had physically and mentally stepped out on me years ago. He never fed me mentally. I never asked it of him—didn't know I needed to make it a requirement.

Now that I have time to reflect on *all* those wasted years, I accept that not requiring Carter to practice certain standards of relationship conduct was one of the ways I let myself down. I allowed myself to live in the lie.

We were the image of the perfect couple without actually living or even believing in what we projected to others. I allowed myself to believe we had something special, but all we had was time.

"Ha," I laughed out loud, my hollow voice bouncing off the walls.

Timothy Carter.

I had done everything in my power to make him happy. I kept our three-bedroom Richmond, Virginia condo immaculately clean. I cooked nearly every day. I maintained my exercise routine religiously to stay cute for him. I planned and hosted parties for him and his friends and events for his employees.

And in the end, Carter gave up on me. Stopped fighting for me. For us. Yet, if he asked me back right now, after having been gone for a month, I believe I was desperate enough to take him back. If for nothing else but to fill in the gaping hole of loneliness he left in my chest.

The sweet elixir of alcohol was the helpful assistant I was currently using to drown my sorrows. My best friends, Dayton Davis and Callie Hendrix, made plans to drag me out of my house tonight and away from my need to linger in the depressing state of mind I couldn't shake.

After being with one man since I was a skinny freshman in college, my current transition back to being single wasn't going well.

I jumped, my shoulders colliding with my ears at the sound of my phone vibrating against my wooden coffee table. The noise cut through my mental pity party. I picked up my phone, unaware of how many times it had rung. I wasn't in the mood to talk but swiped to answer it anyway, more to stop the vibrating grunts it made against the table.

"Hello," I answered, my tone clipped and devoid of enthusiasm.

"Are you ready?"

It was my crazy and lovable bestie Dayton, whose appearance fooled many into thinking she was as innocent as a virgin about to be sacrificed. However, she was anything but what she appeared.

Dayton was a straight-up hellcat. She ate men for lunch, and by the time dinner rolled around, she was ready to devour the next one. She didn't apologize for how she treated men either. Growing up in a house with three older brothers and a father who worked two jobs to keep them all clothed and fed was what shaped Dayton's persona.

We were friends for the same length of time I was with Carter. Dayton, Callie, and I had met in college and have been close friends ever since. Dayton never hesitated to remind me that if Carter wouldn't marry me after all the time we'd been together, he never would. And she'd been right.

"Charla!" I jumped again, this time at Dayton's roaring voice booming through my phone. "Stop thinking about Carter and get ready. And wear something sexy. I don't want you looking like you borrowed an outfit from my grandma tonight."

"Okay," I huffed, knowing she would keep fussing if I didn't answer her.

"If I get there and you're not ready, prepare to be sick of me. You hear me?" she asked.

Dayton couldn't stand Carter, and although she hadn't said it to my face, I knew she was happy about the breakup.

"Loud and clear," I replied. "I'm getting ready now, drill sergeant."

As much as I hated to admit it, Dayton was right about me getting out. A month had gone by in a blur of confusion and anger. And I believe I was feeling more sorry for myself than for the actual loss of the relationship. I needed to accept that Carter wasn't coming back and move the hell on already.

Glancing down, I ran a hand over my chest. My tits barely qualified as C's, so I fished around for one of the hot tops Callie made for me, specifically to put my chest on display. I picked out the black lacy bustier top with silk and mesh that made up the areas that covered my skin.

The material clung, kissing the perfect spots that accentuated my body into a perfect silhouette. It was like wearing an art piece. Besides, it was time someone else reaped the benefits of my workout plan. It was also time I officially labeled Carter my ex.

"Think about something else, Charla," I scolded myself, murmuring under my breath.

I needed to concentrate on the one-night stand I'd been contemplating for the last few weeks. Hopefully, I'll have enough nerve to follow through with it and that it shows me what I was missing out on.

Dayton planted that seed in my head a few days after my ex walked out on me, but I hadn't found the motivation to follow through with the idea until recently.

Glancing down at my ripped jeans, I smiled. The rips in my thigh area were gaping enough to give a good sneak peek of my toned brown thighs. Thankfully, I hadn't let myself completely go. I even kept my appointment at the spa and got my nails and toes taken care of a few days ago.

My thick and lengthy relaxed hair was styled into a fishtail ponytail. It fell past my bra strap, which usually resulted in me getting my hair tugged on by people checking to see if I grew it or purchased it.

I dabbed on my favorite body oil, Secrets of the Desert, behind my ears, on my wrist, and a little on the seam of my jeans in my lower region. After lining my eyes and lips, I applied shiny lip gloss, a few brushes of mascara, and considered myself ready.

My doorbell rang just as I was strapping on one of my heels. Limping to the door in one heel, I swung it open.

Dayton and Callie strutted in and at first glance one would think a famous Hollywood designer dressed them. All polished skin, flawless makeup, and stylish clothes. They were camera-ready worthy.

A silky black halter-top romper highlighted what Dayton deemed her best asset. Her ass. It was entertaining to see how men fell all over themselves trying to peek at her ass, many ignoring that she also had a beautiful face. Her light makeup didn't take away from the innocence people were fooled by.

She paired the outfit with a pair of edgy gold stilettos and a gold belt. Dayton was what some described as high yellow. She was a creamy, light beige that she felt the need to tan, making her the only black woman I knew who paid actual money for UV rays. The results of her tanning gave her a mixed appearance, making it difficult to determine her ethnicity.

Although we never talked about it, I believed Dayton had been traumatized as a result of her light complexion, enough that she believed she needed to darken it. She'd flat-ironed her usual shoulder-length natural curls bone straight so her hair reached midway down her back.

Callie had her own unique style. To my eyes, most of what she wore didn't make sense, but it always worked stylishly. Her sense of fashion worked so well that she was paid to dress an up-and-coming girls' R&B singing group, Twisted Minds, who were making a big splash on the Hollywood scene.

Callie often traveled with the group and was given a budget to shop for and dress them. The group modeled many of the outfits she designed for them, which helped to skyrocket her career.

The outfit Callie was currently wearing was borrowed from the 1980s, a multi-colored polka dot top and a pair of striped torn denim shorts. The legs of the shorts were frayed up her thighs. A pair of ripped fishnet stockings flowed into a pair of high-top Nikes that were probably collectibles. Callie loved pulling from the past to create future styles. She called it her design version of Sankofa.

My friends circled me, inspecting me thoroughly before they allowed approval to flash in their eyes. I hadn't missed that their asses had stepped into my house and hadn't even spoken to me but went straight to inspector mode.

"Glad to see that ten years of being trapped in a monogamous relationship hasn't completely taken away your ability to make yourself look hot. I'd hit it," Dayton commented.

Callie and I shook our heads at Dayton's words. No one knew what would come out of her mouth from one moment to the next.

"You *might* pull attention tonight *if* you can straighten out your face and smile," Callie urged.

I gifted them with a dramatic eye roll before releasing a deep sigh.

"Are you guys done picking on me? Can we leave already?"

My plan was to drink until I was drunk and pretend to be having fun. Nothing or no one would stop Dayton or

Callie from drinking, so we'd ordered an Uber to get us to and from the club.

Tonight was the night that I was putting my big girl panties on and experiencing what a one-night stand felt like. I desperately needed to take advantage of my new-found freedom and pull myself from this hole of despair I'd willingly jumped into. The two ideas, freedom and a one-night stand, were what I kept reminding myself of in order to step out of my own way and attempt to have fun.

Chapter Two

Charla

A strip-club? The realist in me knew that not all strippers were bad boys, bad people, or sex-crazed fanatics. However, I would be lying if I said I didn't find it difficult to give them the benefit of the doubt.

Why was I being judgmental for no reason? My no-man-having-ass needed to chill and concentrate on allowing myself to accept and give joy, if only for a few hours.

The strippers in this establishment must have been something special based on the number of impatient women waiting in line to get inside. We endured the gum-popping, complaint-evoking, gossip festival in the line for nearly forty minutes before we even arrived at the front door.

The minimum age of entry was twenty-five, and us being carded for looking younger was a compliment and a great start to the evening. Dayton received extra attention concerning her age. Her innocent face, despite her curvy body, made the hosts at the door suspicious enough to confer with one of his buddies, both eyeing her ID and her seriously before they allowed us entry.

The music when we first stepped inside was set at a tolerable level so you only had to slightly raise your voice to talk to the person next to you versus yelling at their face. The first view of the inside waiting area revealed designer furniture pieces and classy wall art that gave the place the feel of the inside of a high-classed mansion.

This club was a hell of a lot classier than I expected. A large gold and white marble staircase greeted us as soon as we pushed through the large hardwood double doors and stepped across the threshold into the main floor area. Marble finishes were apparently a staple in this place. The cracked-marble floors sparkled like glass under large, expensive Persian rugs. Porcelain white statues of godlike men and goddess women in erotic positions were displayed throughout the room. Despite the erotic nature, the art was tasteful enough to spark intrigue. Expensive presentations of inanimate art you couldn't identify highlighted other areas.

We strutted past the wide staircase, our heels clicking and blending with the music, laughter, and vocal exchanges of the mingling crowd. A large, raised stage sat off in the distance, with lights angled across the top of the dark burgundy curtains blanketing the area.

The place was a feast for the eyes. Two large and well-stocked bars sat to the left and right of the stage and far enough away so that women were allowed easy access to gather around the stage at show time.

Smaller performing areas for dancers to highlight their bodies and dance moves were set up throughout the area. A few areas were set in cozy corners, the atmosphere giving off an alluring vibe to cater to women's desires. It didn't matter where you sat—you were going to be close to hot male action.

We stepped in further, allowing ourselves to be swallowed by the crowd and consumed by the opulence of the place. I couldn't tell that the floor sloped downward until my feet wobbled in my heels and reminded me to be more mindful of my steps toward our destination. The auditorium effect afforded those furthest from the stage a good view.

All of the chairs on the main floor had already been taken. The only empty seats were a series of neatly set tables at the corners of the stage. The nameplates sitting in the center of the tables marked them as reserved.

Busy taking in the scenery, I absently followed Callie, who followed Dayton. Although I'd heard of this club, Quiet Chaos, I had never seen it in person and always pictured it as a P-Valley or Player's Club-type scene. My assumption couldn't have been more wrong.

A flash of movement in the corner of my eye snatched my attention, giving me the answer to where the fancy marble stairs led. Another bar was on the upper deck. The expanse of the top level was open so you could view the stage and dancers from above.

"That's the VIP section. You can get lap dances, take pictures, and lord knows what else with the dancers up there," Callie informed me.

I took in the reserved tables on our level again because I believed we were headed toward them. The area near the stage looked more like the VIP section, but I couldn't accurately see all that was offered upstairs.

I vaguely made out a different vibe of music playing on the top level and spotted a few women with VIP badges around their necks glancing down at us. I nodded my approval of the place to no one in particular and was unable to help smiling.

Many of the women in attendance were dressed to impress in expensive dresses, casual wear, and some similar to me and Callie in jeans. The more the scene unfolded, the more I began to appreciate the class the environment exuded with its plush seating arrangements.

Were the men as classy as their place of employment? Apparently, my question was about to be answered because the stage lights gradually brightened, and the curtains fluttered to life.

The volume of the crowd's tone dulled to low murmurs and even a *shush* here and there sounded.

"Our table is over here, ladies. We're sharing with another group of women I know from work," Dayton announced as she pointed us to the table sitting off to the right of the stage. It was positioned so you could remain seated and still have a good view of the stage.

Thankfully, there was no space for others to jump in front of us unless they climbed on top of the table. This place was designed so you wouldn't miss a view of the action.

"Callie and Charla, this is Leslie, Brenda, and Fiona," Dayton introduced us to the rest of the table. We shared smiles and handshakes, and based on their energy, the ladies were eager for the dancers to get started. The large stacks of bills I noticed in their hands was another indication.

My eyes bucked at the sight of the stacks of fives and tens Leslie and Fiona clutched. I hadn't been to a strip club since my twenty-first birthday eight years ago when we were handing out singles.

Scanning the area, I noticed stacks of money being withdrawn from every imaginable space, including bras. I didn't bring a purse, much less a stack of money. All I had in my possession was my driver's license, a debit card, and three-twenties. I glanced around the space for a place to exchange the bills for singles.

I was in full observation mode by the time I noticed that the light tap on my arm wasn't from the beat of the music. It was Callie. My head swiveled in her direction to find a stack of fives about an inch thick being handed over to me. My lips fell apart at the sight of what had to have been a thousand bucks.

"Happy Birthday! We love you," came Callie and Dayton's excited voices.

A quick smile creased my lips. I knew them well enough not to argue about the amount of money they expected me to waste on a stranger I'd never see again. Instead, I graciously accepted the money with a wide smile. A rush of emotions hit me, and I was forced to hold back the tears stinging my eyes.

"Thank you, ladies. I love you guys, too."

I stood and shamelessly drew them into a group hug, squeezing them together hard enough to make them squeal. My lip gloss was left on Callie's cheek since she was the lucky recipient closest to my lips. Dayton dodged my attack.

My current status had been set on emotional wreck lately, so they didn't hold it against me when I got all mushy. The only people in the world I openly shared my feelings with were my friends. Unmarried at twenty-eight, twenty-nine in a few hours, I would have been cast off as an old maid back in the day. I cast the depressing idea away.

By the time I took my seat, a statuesque woman with Native American features stepped onto the stage. Her shimmery gold dress showed off her impressive figure and could have easily been a part of a top designer's secret stash. It definitely wasn't from the off-the-rack variety of clothing I was used to purchasing.

Not that I couldn't afford better, but I enjoyed piecing together outfits I was often complimented on from various department stores. However, the most unique pieces of clothing I owned had been created by Callie.

The lighting was turned up only for them to start dimming again, successfully regaining the crowd's attention. Out of nowhere, a thundering rumble began, and a herd of shadows appeared to be attacking each other throughout the space.

When thin glimmers of light liberated my vision from the darkness, I found that the erratic movement was a stampede of women running to the stage. A quick glance at Dayton and Callie showed them standing, their eyes glued to the stage.

I'm sure I was the only woman who remained relaxed in my seat. The intro music started, pumping at an ear-rattling beat that drove the crowd wild and even kicked up my energy. *This was going to be a good night*, I told myself.

Chapter Three

Charla

When the music abruptly stopped, breaths were held, and you could hear a pin drop. Eager eyes were locked on the stage. The spotlight surrounded the statuesque emcee in the gold dress.

"Ladies of class, ladies of excellence, society ladies, hardworking ladies, career ladies, welcome to Quiet Chaos!" she announced, her tone vibrating with intense energy. "Are you ready to let your hair down, or better yet, have your hair blown back?"

A synchronized "Yes!" came from the crowd, followed by loud whistles and lust-ridden cheers.

"We have a spectacular line-up for you tonight, including a surprise guest star dancer from our Chicago location."

Energetic cheers heightened to decibels that threatened to blow the roof off the building. Ladies whisper-yelled at each other, wide-eyed and jumpy over the surprise guest.

The emcee waited until it quieted before she spoke again. It appeared everyone in the building knew who this special guest star was, except me.

"Among tonight's line-up are three of our superstars. You ladies know who I'm talking about, right?"

"Hell yes!" The ladies yelled, receiving teasing head gestures from the pleased emcee.

I was reasonably excited, but I couldn't find the switch to flip that would allow me to express it. I faked my level of excitement to match the room with exaggerated smiles that I bet had me looking like the Joker from

Batman. Not to mention, I'm sure I resembled a baby seal, clapping when I should have been shouting.

"Hallelujah," I said under my breath when the drinks we ordered before the stampede broke out finally arrived. I ordered a top-shelf Long Island Iced Tea. My plan was to get as tipsy as possible so I would at least get a good night's sleep out of this deal.

A one-night stand would be the perfect ending to my night, but it was probably out of the question in this group. With the level of aggressive and confident women in this crowd, the likelihood of me going home with one of the dancers like I daydreamed about was next to impossible.

I glanced up from my drink when a second wave of ladies dashed toward the stage. Callie, Dayton, and the rest of our table were among the crowd, preferring to have some reach advantage added to their view.

Dayton attempted to drag me along when she took off but lost her grip on my arm when I didn't make an attempt to move. I was fine with enjoying the view from our table.

The emcee allowed her gaze to meander over the crowd before she introduced the first dancer.

"This is his second month with us here at Quiet Chaos, but he already has panties melting. Ladies, I present to you the magically delicious D-Trix!"

When D-Trix walked out on the stage, the noise level shot up so high that I vibrated along with the drink in my glass. He wore a full magician's suit with the top hat and all. The music was the Lucky Charms theme music backed up by a booty-shaking beat.

When D-Trix asked for a volunteer to be his assistant, the women went wilder than they already were. He took his time finding the woman he wanted. Once he had her on stage, he picked her up, caveman style, before sitting her atop his large display box.

The music changed to a darker, more mysterious song I didn't recognize as the lights dimmed, and one was left bright to highlight the dancer and his lucky assistant. The scene kept my interest, and D-Trix executed several impressive magic tricks to start his performance, pulling red roses from various parts of his gracious volunteer's body.

He didn't pull a rabbit out of his hat, but he made you believe that he'd withdrawn a dozen roses from between the woman's legs. Each time he performed a trick, he took a piece of clothing off his body while showcasing his impressive dance moves.

The man was a beautiful feast for my eyes. Perfectly tanned skin, low cropped dark hair, toned to perfection without an ounce of fat on his six foot plus and at least two-twenty pound body. However, his face *did* look young. With my eyes fixated on him, it occurred to me that he had put thought, time, and effort into his performance.

He wasn't only an impressively well-built and good-looking man, he had an actual noteworthy talent, pulling off the act of disappearing and making his volunteer reappear in front of him in the doggy-style position.

When he made his dick move at will and spank the woman on the ass with no hands, all of his other tricks were forgotten. By the time D-Trix finished his performance, the women around the stage were at his mercy and swooning when he closed out his segment in nothing but a G-string that covered his hard, large magic stick.

His influence over the women had been so strong that he'd encouraged them to decorate the stage with an insane amount of green money. He finished off his performance by disappearing in a puff of blue smoke.

The drink was putting me in a more contented state of mind. I clapped and cheered boisterously from my seat. When I noticed the waitress placing drinks on the table next to ours, I raised my drink and pointed at my glass. She acknowledged me with a head nod before taking off and heading toward the bar to my left.

Dayton and Callie had insisted on paying for everything tonight. I already decided the money they gave me to throw away on these men would also be put to good use, paying for the drinks I didn't plan to stop ordering. As a matter of fact, I planned to tell the waiter to keep them coming every twenty minutes until it was time for us to leave.

My friends and I weren't *financially embarrassed* as Dayton liked to say, but I wasn't one to waste money, not when I could be paying it forward to a better cause.

I was a senior-level accountant for one of the best firms in the city, Rex, Shaw, & Anders. Callie was an up-and-coming designer. Dayton, although she acted like a man trapped in a woman's body, was a Nurse Practitioner. The only thing we couldn't nail down were good men.

I loved Carter, but I was never *in* love with him. I didn't believe in that type of love and had never revealed to my friends the depth of my true emotions for Carter. It took him leaving for me to accept that I would never be head over heels in love with him.

I couldn't help thinking that Carter knew or sensed as much, and it may have been why he'd never put a ring on my finger. We were each other's comfort. Nothing more than a well-placed convenience to each other.

Carter filled a spot. One I would have gladly let him fill for the rest of my life. It would have saved me from having to wade through these man-troubled waters to find a replacement. Carter's departure had hurt me, but it wasn't a broken heart I was suffering from. It was being left to start over. The fear of going through the motions of trying to find the right man to fit into my spaces, mental and physical, wasn't something I believed I'd ever have to do again.

Deep into my second drink and feeling *nice*, the fourth dancer was about to hit the stage. I enjoyed the first two dancers and half paid attention to the third, who came out dressed like a postman.

Although the postman issued the women packages, each containing actual gifts, there was only one package that drew the women's interest. Now that I was tipsy, I didn't have a care in the world.

"You're going to get a great tip," I announced to the waitress when she placed my third drink in front of me and took my watered-down second drink from the table. When I lifted my drink to my lips, my eyes connected with the dancer on the stage.

He was announced as The Assassin, one of the super-stars the emcee had mentioned earlier. He began the routine in a full black ninja costume, and each piece he peeled off had tongues wagging.

Was it wishful thinking on my part, or was he staring directly at me as he ground his pelvis into the stage floor? He pulled two women onto the stage and used them as his props to show us some martial arts moves. The way he twisted, turned, and danced around their bodies, I was sure they would have come three times already if any part of them had been penetrated.

I turned my head over my right and left shoulder to make sure I wasn't imagining that this perfectly tanned man was looking at me. Clean-shaven with a jawline you wanted to lick, I was riveted to *him*, not his performance. I sat my drink down when he licked his lips and winked at me. The eye wink broke me out of the haze I was in while staring at him.

The Assassin stood at least six-foot-four, and his medium frame was toned to perfection but not overly muscled with the huge bulges that left men looking like aliens versus humans. His short, cropped hair was a dark, dirty blond and just long enough to slide my fingers through. Good-looking, kissable, deep pink lips. There was nothing about this man you didn't want to kiss or caress.

Another piece of his outfit, a sword and metal fighting stars that appeared to be real, came off. The sight enticed me to want to see more, a lot more. If there was such a thing as walking sin, this was him in the flesh.

He had the kind of appearance and build that would make you abandon what you knew to be right and embrace the dark side. The man had some stalkers, I'm sure. Staring at him made me want to do all sorts of wrong.

He should rename himself Hypnotic because he had me under whatever spell he was casting up there on that stage. The sweat from my cold glass slid over my fingers and served up a small reminder of where I was and what these men's jobs were. They provided a woman with her fantasy, whatever that might be.

I didn't even have to glance around to know that every pair of eyes was on this man. They likely fantasized about taking him home and letting him have his way, or was it only me having those types of erotic thoughts?

When The Assassin performed b-boy, break dancing, and more martial arts moves mixed with that sexy stripper flare, the crowd went crazy.

The women didn't make it rain money—they caused a torrential downpour that had the stage flooded with green bills. I couldn't ignore this man's sex appeal. He made me want to throw the whole bundle of fives my friends gave me onto the stage, just for keeping my attention and pulling me out of my own depressing state of mind.

I never considered dating outside my race because I was with one man my entire adult life. However, if I met this man under a different set of circumstances and he approached me with interest, the decision would be an easy one.

Although my eyes refused to drop away from *my* Assassin, I lifted my drink and started sipping again. The Assassin did his thing and continued to wet every pair of panties in the building. His movements flowed to the beat and automatically conjured up images of him fucking me with the same sexy moves.

He pulled a third woman onto the stage and performed an acrobatic dance routine that simulated him having slow, deep, impacting sex with all of them. The moves alone likely gave them each an automatic orgasm and made the crowd lose their minds.

One of the ladies on stage appeared to be swooning, and I wasn't altogether sure she was faking. Another of them kept her hand over her heart like it was about to burst out of her chest cavity. He didn't forget about involving the crowd in the sexually charged routine. If The Assassin did half the moves in real life as he was on that stage, he was a walking sexual goldmine.

Several ladies at the edge of the stage lifted their purses up, letting him know he could do whatever he wanted to their finances. It made me laugh at how far this guy had gotten into their minds. He could make this crowd do anything he asked of them.

The realist in me decided to rear her ugly head, reminding me that I was not going to let any of these overly-manicured men trick me into believing they wanted me. Hell, there was an ocean of willing and beautiful women for them to choose from, so why would any of them even glance in my direction?

My hot and cold vibes alone would be like a repellent to the opposite sex. I was getting sick of myself. Why couldn't I just get over myself already?

As soon as The Assassin exited the stage, I stood on wobbly legs and waited until my balance realigned before I headed to the bathroom. It would take them time to pick up all the money The Assassin earned, so this was the perfect time to take a break.

Woozy on my legs, I took careful steps on my way to the nearest restroom. It was like I was gliding instead of stepping, a clear indication that tipsy had officially taken control of my functions.

I literally peed a river, and by the time I exited, the two restrooms had lines of women waiting to release all that alcohol they had consumed. While approaching our table I noticed, Dayton, Callie, and the rest of the crew had returned. Each sipped on new drinks and eyeballed me like I had three heads.

Callie grabbed my arm and snatched my tipsy ass closer. She appeared to be unaware that she was handling me with her bitch strength.

"Girl, they said one of the dancers ordered these drinks for us. The waitress left you another one. She said the mystery dancer said to bring us whatever we wanted for the rest of the night."

Dayton threw in her two cents. "Somebody at this table has impressed someone tonight, and I hope it was me. You guys know I'm taking one of these men home tonight and using him up until he can't move anymore."

I shook my head, releasing a burst of laughter at Dayton because I didn't doubt she would do exactly as she said if one of these men were fool enough to go home with her. When it came to relationships, Dayton was *challenged.*

She wanted nothing to do with being tied down to a man. To drive that point home, she rarely slept with the same man twice unless the dick was so good, she had to test it again to make sure she wasn't exaggerating the experience.

At this point, the drinks had me sitting there bouncing back and forth between cloud nine and ten. My heavy eyes danced all over the table as I laughed at comments that weren't even funny. My friends hadn't confronted me yet about babysitting the table, but I was sure their tough-love pep talk would be coming soon.

As soon as the emcee stepped back onto the stage, sporting a silk yellow dress this time, every lady from my table raced toward the stage in a mad dash to get the best spot. The only move I made was to reach down for my drink.

I had no intention of going up there, and it surprised me that Callie and Dayton left me again without scolding me for keeping my distance from the hot men, one of which I was supposed to be convincing to take me home and fuck my brains out.

Yeah. Right.

I giggled to myself, attempting to take a sip, but the straw missed my numb bottom lip.

We had been here for just over an hour, but it felt like it had been twelve. I was beyond ready to go at this point because the alcohol had heightened my need to close my heavy eyes and fall into a deep, drunken sleep.

Chapter Four

Charla

A burst of warm energy flowed over me when I placed my hand over my mouth to yawn. The shadow of a tall frame loomed at my back, but I ignored the presence, figuring it was another drunk person, lost or mingling.

When the presence refused to move out of my space or away from my table, I glanced back and caught the sight of a pair of expensive-looking slip-ons. My glance shot up jean-clad legs that were about a mile high and a plain white t-shirt that clung to a medium, strong, and sturdy frame.

My gaze froze on the handsome face smiling above me. He looked familiar, but I was unable to recall where I'd seen him before. If the women weren't concentrating on what gyrated on the stage, they would likely mistake this man for one of the dancers.

Wait.

He *is* one of the dancers. I finally made the connection.

"Finally, I get acknowledged." The smooth tone of his voice cut through the music and stroked me like an exploring hand.

"May I join you, please?" he asked. His tone was warm silk sliding over my skin. When I thought the man couldn't get any sexier, his voice made me a liar. My entangled thoughts straighten themselves out long enough for me to recall his question.

Why the hell did he want to join me? Couldn't he see that I planned to drink myself into a sleep coma?

The little tipsy and slurring voice in my head reminded me: *He's doing his job, working the room to get every dollar in the building.*

Since this guy was awaiting my response, I ushered my head toward the chair next to mine, using my foot to put a little space between our chairs before he sat. He noticed and smiled, his gaze zipping over the seat before his laughter sounded.

He leaned too far into my personal space for my liking when he took the seat and dragged it right back into place next to mine. He kept scooting closer, causing the chair to vibrate under his shifting weight.

His fresh scent wasn't one you could easily ignore. It was like warm, clean linen in a battle with his cologne for dominance. It was the kind of freshness drenched in a lively warmth you wanted to keep inhaling.

I jerked my neck back and cast a mean side eye at him when he leaned way too close to my face. He maintained his position, ignoring my attempt to distance. His sexy lips were near my ear, so I had no trouble deciphering his words or enjoying his warm breath sweeping over my lobe.

"What's your name?"

Why on earth was he trying to talk to me—the one woman in the building who didn't want to be bothered? I was content sitting there dating my drinks while casually glancing up at the mostly naked men on the stage. After a quick intake of air, I released a deep sigh. I'm sure most of my alcohol-scented breath blew in his face.

"I don't mean to be rude, but I am not interested. I was dumped a month ago, and I'm still angry enough about it to take my frustrations out on you."

"I wouldn't mind," he said, scooting his damn chair even closer. "As a matter of fact, we can help each other. I have a different kind of agony I'm trying to escape."

His damn voice. His scent. I'd be damned if it wasn't affecting me. To say this guy was handsome was the understatement of the century. Was my rude attitude having some kind of positive affect on this man?

"By the way, whoever dumped you is likely someplace kicking his own ass for making such a foolish mistake."

The statement had my lips attempting to turn up into a cheesy smile. I knew it was a line he fed me, but I liked hearing it anyway.

My gaze, after it took a stroll over his body, finally landed back on his face, and our eyes locked. This man wasn't just handsome. I couldn't recall ever seeing a man who was so damned deliciously put together.

He was the kind of neat handsomeness that let you know that he invested a lot of time in himself. He made a simple pair of jeans look like they belonged in a magazine. Although the setting was dim, it didn't hide his impressive jawline that had my gaze chasing the clean-shaven razor's edge of it.

His eyes were a brilliant mix of greens and yellows that drew me into their alluring depths. Those lips of his were the sexiest I had seen on a man. Full, plush, and lickable. I wouldn't have minded those lips on every part of me. Even his nose, though it bore a slight slant to the right, was sexy in a manly way.

His body. *Whew!* His body was a sinfully crafted work of art. Although he was fully clothed, any woman in her right mind would have to fight to keep from admiring him. He was also giving off enough big dick energy that you didn't have to see him on that stage to know he was concealing a lethal weapon.

My eyes completed another revolution around his universe, scanning his body. My mind returned to my brain so I could continue rejecting him in the hopes that it would continue to have a positive effect on him. He reached out his hand.

"Ransome."

His hand hung in the air, forcing me to drop my gaze from his face to take it. When I finally took his hand, I expected a quick shake and release, but not from Mr. Handsome. He held tightly to my hand and wouldn't release it. His warm, firm flesh cushioned my hand, making it tingle. He kept my hand in his grip, rubbing his thumb tenderly along the back.

"You plan on telling me your name?" he questioned in that sexy timbre of his.

"What's the point?"

His eyebrows shot up at my clipped comment.

"Whatever you may think of us dancers, some of us are lonely people. Some of us are also misunderstood."

He managed to say it with sincerity in his eyes after he'd almost made three women come on stage without taking a stitch of clothing off of them. He must have taken my non-response for an actual response to his comment about being misunderstood, so he elaborated.

"Male dancers. We are not all womanizing assholes who sleep around with everyone who catches our attention. Nor do we have harems of women at our disposal."

"Is that right?" I asked, the sarcasm dripping in thick droplets from my lips.

"As a matter of fact. The last three women I attempted to date seriously couldn't mentally get past my job long enough to see *me*. They couldn't see that I truly intended to forge a serious relationship."

My heavy gaze raked over his face. It was likely written all over my unimpressed glare that I didn't believe a word he said either.

"Well, if you ask me, it's not worth it to immerse yourself fully in one person only to have them dump you when times get tough. If that's the case, you're the lucky one. I'm tired of being the good girl, tired of always doing what I'm supposed to, sticking by my man even though I was never truly *in* love with him. To give him ten stress-free years. To cook for him. To clean for him. To sacrifice time and some of my goals and dreams for him. To have him not only cheat on me and get someone else pregnant, and up and leave me out of the blue on top of it."

My eyes slammed shut after my rant. I slapped my hands over my mouth to stop myself from going any further. I'd just spilled all my baggage on a stranger. The shame in allowing this man a glimpse at how pathetic I'd allowed myself to get made my face go hot with embarrassment. What happened to the confidence I'd painstakingly built and embraced earlier?

A deep breath didn't release me from the tension of my shame. I needed to find a way to piece myself back together because it was obvious being comfortable with Carter had forced me to check out of my own life.

A random idea popped into my brain as my lazy gaze scanned the hot man sitting next to me, with sympathy and concern flashing in his gaze. I hadn't even noticed he had placed his big, warm hand over mine on the table until he moved it, rubbing tenderly over my skin. Was I seeing what I wanted to see, or was that genuine care reflected in his gaze?

Maybe I *was* drunk enough to do something stupid. If my depressing rant about being dumped wasn't enough to chase away sexy Mr. Ransome, then I may get the day-dream I cast off as an impossibility. However, I found myself at a loss for words and feared I would embarrass myself further if I kept talking.

I took a couple of sips from my drink and glanced at the stage. The dancer below the flashing lights stripped out of a lion's costume. His scene was jungle-inspired, and he had two women on stage locked in sexual captivity.

Ransome's sexy voice drew my attention back to him.

"If what you had with the ex-boyfriend didn't work for you, try something different," he said, squeezing his big hand over the top of mine. "Don't be the good girl anymore. Do what makes *you* feel good. Do whatever the hell it is that suits your needs."

A loud burst of laughter shot out of my mouth, followed by a low burp.

"You have no idea how close you've come to nailing how I've been feeling lately. My intent was to come out tonight with my friends, find a man I'd like to take home, screw him, and never talk to him again. But I couldn't get drunk enough for my brain to put the plan into action."

"I'd like to volunteer. I'd gladly go home with you, and I'd let you do whatever you want with me."

Why the hell was this man so intent on making my foolish behavior into a reality? I stared at him long and hard. Based on the sternness in his unblinking gaze, he was dead ass serious.

As if reading my mind, he stated, "I'm serious. Take me home with you."

I believed him. Was I too drunk to be making this kind of decision? I didn't believe this guy was working me over for the stack of fives I had in my possession. He hadn't asked me for anything other than my company.

"Ransome," I called out, glad I remembered his name and finding that it was too nice a name to forget. "If you're serious, find me at the end of the show, and I'll take you home."

I aimed a finger at my friends hanging over the stage, one on either side of the dancer, shoving money down his G-string.

"My friends aren't going to leave this place until the last sexually explicit move has been executed, so I'm stuck here until then."

Ransome shook his head. "I don't want you to get away from me, so I don't mind sitting here with you until then." He leaned in so close, I inhaled a whiff of his fresh breath, the warmth of it caressing my earlobe. "Will you please give me your name?"

"What's the point?" I maintained a stiff side-eye. "If we follow through with this plan of ours, I'll never see you again after tonight."

His infectious smile was highlighted by straight white teeth. The hint of genuine honesty in his expression drew more of my attention.

"Even if it's only for one night, I still want to know your name."

"Charla, short for Charlene," I finally answered.

Interest?

Was I reading him all wrong? There was genuine interest in the depth of his gaze. He really didn't care about me being a little prickly. I think he liked it because it was the opposite of the way he was normally treated by women, especially in this club.

I shook off what my brain attempted to convince me of. The nice blend of Tequila, White rum, Triple Sec, and Vodka was doing its job and had me seeing what I wanted to see in those mesmerizing green eyes.

For all I knew, the man could resemble a zoo animal, and my drunk mind had me seeing a god among men. I prayed I wouldn't wake up lying next to a gorilla.

"Thank you, Charla. We're going to have fun," he assured, giving my hand a light squeeze since his was still splayed over mine.

Was I agreeing to let this unbelievably good-looking man take me home? Had Carter hurt me bad enough to follow through with this plan?

While my friends were at the stage having the time of their lives, I was setting up my first booty call.

When Ransome steered our conversation away from hooking up and began telling me about the goals he set for himself, I was a little thrown off but went with it.

His aimed was to successfully transition from stripping to investing more time to his business, a barber shop he either owned or was interested in owning. I didn't know if he was lying or not, but the notion that he was preparing to switch to a more respectful profession was a plus.

Callie had managed to make it onto the stage with a vampire, who attempted to drink blood from the vein he pointed out in her neck and one in her inner thigh.

"I told the bartender earlier that I'll take care of the drinks for you and your friends. I'll go and do that and wait for you at the bar." He leaned his head down and stared into my eyes to make sure I acknowledged him.

I nodded but felt a lot less brave than I had when I'd agreed to take him home earlier.

The light stroke of his fingers traced my shoulder and sent a chill up my spine. The tender stroke had me tracking his movements on the short distance to the bar. Now that I knew who'd offered to buy our drinks, I questioned if he truly made a connection with me while he was dancing.

I craned my neck to see him over dancing women who were holding up and shaking money at the nearest hot male body willing to entertain them. Ransome reached into his back pocket, extracted a credit card from his wallet, and handed it to the bartender.

He took a seat in one of the vacated barstools and waited. I returned his wave when he glanced back and caught me staring after him.

Minutes later, the ladies made their way back to our table, but none took their seats. Dayton's work friends bid us a quick good night and took off. Callie and Dayton stood to either side of me, waiting for me to get up, I supposed.

When the lights were turned fully on, and the music lowered, it was our cue that it was time to go. The statement, *you ain't gotta go home, but you got to get the hell outta here*, came to mind.

I stood on unsteady legs. Before I could tell my friends my plan to let a handsome stranger take me home, he was there, standing next to me. His warm hand rested on my lower back.

"Ladies, this is Ransome. He's agreed to take me home."

The lights highlighted Ramson's features. He was even more beautiful up close. The blinding stage light and the dim club setting, in my opinion, didn't accurately depict his true depth.

I had been right about those gorgeous eyes of his, too. Subtle flecks of yellow sparkled in his light green gaze. His eye color added an edge to his look when combined with his evenly tanned skin. He was astonishingly handsome, a perfect mix of features compiled from a group of women's fantasies.

The pride-filled expression and wide smile on Dayton's face wasn't missed, but Callie's stressed expression revealed reluctance, especially when she caught Ransome not so conspicuously checking me out in the better lighting. A deep smile teased his lips before Callie's mean glare captured his attention.

"Don't worry, ladies. I am a responsible adult. I rarely drink, and I will make sure Charla gets home safe and sound."

"Okay," Dayton said with authority. "Anything happens to my friend. I know where you work, and trust me, I won't hesitate to fuck up your world if I hear one complaint from her."

Ransome lifted his hands. "I've got this. You're not going to have to fuck up my world."

Callie hugged me first. She wobbled in my hold, and I didn't know if she was tipsy or had to pee. Her lips didn't hover at my ear but sat atop my lobe.

Tipsy.

"Make sure you have mace ready if he tries something you don't like, and hit me on speed dial if you need me."

I pressed a quick peck on her cheek without replying. She knew I also had a gun that I knew how to use, thanks to the dreaded ex I was attempting to get over. Not only that, but I always kept my self-defense skills fresh. If all else failed, I would scream my ass off and run like hell.

Dayton's embrace was in direct contrast to Callie's. She leaned her head against the side of mine so her lips were right at my ear.

"It's about time you give it up to someone else. Make sure you use him *real* good. Do *everything* you think I would do and then some."

Her instructions left me laughing and pulling away from her in a playful gesture to save myself from the madness she gave off. My friends were crazy, but they were more than friends—they were my family.

I grew up with a single mother, who died from cancer a few weeks after I left for Saint Augustine University. My mother had been battling cancer for three years and had never revealed it to me.

I never saw any telltale signs. No medicines, extra doctor's appointments that I was aware of, and no drastic changes to her appearance. I believe she forced herself to live to see me turn eighteen. She pushed hard enough to see me through my graduation and first days of college.

Huge shit-eating grins were tossed over their shoulders while Dayton and Callie stepped away. I remained standing next to my living nightcap.

His hand touched down on the center of my back and slid until it remained resting on my lower back. He led me past the stairs and toward the exit. His light stroke along my back was enough to keep me warm and interested to see how the rest of the night would turn out.

The shuffle of enthusiastically drunk women exiting the building had died down, and the crowd had thinned considerably. The remaining women eyeballed Ransome but didn't approach. His hand on me must have been the warning they needed to keep their distance.

When we arrived at a white Mercedes 500 series, it was a surprise, but at the same time, I knew Ransome could afford it based on how sensibly he talked about transiting from a stripper to a legit business owner.

He hit his key fob to open the door and walked me to the passenger side. My eyebrows shot up quickly when he opened my door and helped me inside.

This move was unexpected. I never received this level of chivalry from my ex, and rarely from other men, I considered a part of our circle.

"Thank you," I told him appreciatively before I sank into his black, plush leather seat and rested my head against the headrest.

Was Ransome being chivalrous to impress me, or was this a part of his *real* personality? Why was I even thinking about it? We were about to go to my place, offload our sins, and never see each other again. .

Chapter Five

Ransome

Eyes closed and head thrown back against the headrest, Charla appeared relaxed, rolling with me in my car. Her posture indicated a certain level of trust, unknowingly or not, in me. Considering her recent relationship issues, I didn't expect her to be so calm. She may have also been experiencing the effects of the four-and-a-half drinks she consumed.

What would she think of me if she knew I'd had my eyes on her from the moment she stepped into the club? A small section behind the stage allowed us to peek into the club unseen.

Instantly, my eyes zeroed in on her, and my mind refused to give her up. I didn't take her for a heavy drinker, but based on what she revealed about the way her relationship had ended, she was entitled to the temporary diversion.

Before we stepped out of the club, I spotted doubt in her gaze and prayed she didn't start second-guessing her decision to take me home.

"Address, please," I chimed, my fingers waiting to program her address into my navigation system.

A silent moment stretched out so long that I feared she'd changed her mind until she finally began calling out a number followed by the street address name.

"800 Cobblestone Circle."

The smile that started at the giving of her address remained like a permanent fixture on my face while following the direction of the monotone female voice flowing through the speakers. My eyes neglected the road because they preferred being on Charla. This was the first time I was drawn so intensely to a woman. The stimulating connection scared me but excited me more.

Even in the dim setting at the club, my attention was pulled in her direction. After the lights came on, I was more impressed with the way she looked, as well as her unshakable vibe that radiated a sense of positivity despite our surroundings. Not even her mood over her recent breakup had dulled the shine of the radiant air I picked up from her.

"Charla, you're a beautiful woman."

At my words, she lifted her head from the headrest and smiled, but her eyes remained closed like she savored the compliment.

"There is something about you that calls to me with this vibrance and calming ease I can't explain. And I'm not feeding you a line. The simplest way to put it, I'm just into you."

Her eyes popped open, but she didn't glance in my direction. She allowed herself a moment to digest my words.

"Thank you."

Her words were low, unsure. I believe I scared her by speaking so freely about a connection that very well could have been one-sided. I couldn't eloquently explain to her why I wanted her. I just did. I believed I needed her and she may even need me, but explaining what I sensed would sound crazy.

"Tell me about yourself, Charla. And, please, don't give me the line about us *not* seeing each other anymore after tonight. If anything, the knowledge that you won't be seeing me again should encourage you to tell me anything. Whatever you may want to get off your chest."

According to the navigation system, we had twenty-one miles to travel, and with the heavy 1-64 traffic, we would likely be on the road for an hour. It took Charla a few silent miles to warm up to the idea of sharing herself with me, but all that mattered was that she eventually did.

"I'm an accountant for a well-established firm here in the city. The work is demanding but rewarding. I work a lot of overtime. I used to try not to allow work to take away all of my personal time, but now it's all that keeps me from obsessing about what's going on in my personal life."

She paused, swallowed.

"I'd been with *him* since I was nineteen, so being alone now feels more like I'm being sentenced for a crime I didn't commit when it should feel like freedom."

As much as I hated to interrupt, I had to ask.

"I know you said he cheated, but you also said he was the one who left you. Does that mean that you forgave him for cheating? Why did he leave you if he was the one doing wrong?"

I refused to accept the notion that any man in his right frame of mind could leave a woman like Charla. Her presence didn't send up red flags, and whether she believed it or not, she was my ideal fantasy woman. Based on her job, she was also well-educated. The pieces she gave me concerning her failed relationship left me baffled.

The pause that followed my questions gave infinity a run for its money. She moved, adjusting herself in the seat before she eventually restarted.

"In a way, I understand why he felt the need to leave, but it hurts just the same. I couldn't give him the one thing he'd been wanting for years. I couldn't give him a child. We tried everything, but it was difficult for me to carry past the first trimester. I even interviewed a few women who were willing to be our surrogate, but he nixed that idea. He said it was too extreme, but little did I know, he'd already gone out and gotten someone else pregnant."

I hadn't expected her to be that open. She folded her hands across her lap before she began to wring them nervously. The hurt she carried made her body slouch. The situation had hit her hard and had her doubting her true worth.

"Did you want kids?"

Her neck jerked in my direction at the question. The tension in her body evaporated, and she relaxed, her shoulders dropping once she let the question sink in.

"It sounds like you were trying for him, but what about you? Did you want kids?" I reiterated.

She shrugged before fingering her forehead.

"I've always wanted children. The idea of being a mother after finding out it wouldn't be easy became a dream I needed to fulfill. To have a mini version of myself, a part of me that I helped to create, would be an amazing accomplishment, something I would have been proud to do, even with him."

Even with him.

The more she talked about her ex, the more I became convinced that she had settled for him. I don't believe he was what she truly wanted in a man, but she had somehow convinced herself he was enough.

"However, I do my best to think realistically," she continued. "After I found out I may never be able to have a baby, I accepted the reality of never being blessed with the gift of motherhood. Despite what I accepted in my heart, I continued to try—for him."

The straight-ahead stare and her clenching hands in her lap spoke for the hurt she suffered. She was fighting her demons and experiencing every emotion while doing it. I reached over and sat my hand over hers and found them shaking. This situation affected her more than she was letting on, but I believed she needed to let all of those emotions filter through her if she was ever going to move on with her life. I just prayed she would find me worthy enough to move on with.

"Some things aren't meant to be Charla. What if you're the right mom and he wasn't the right father? You said you were told you'd have a difficult time having a baby, but did the doctor tell you that you never could?"

She simply stared at me before a small smile surfaced and bloomed into a big grin that lit up her beautiful face.

"You're very perceptive, aren't you?" It was a statement phased like a question that made me smile. All that mattered to me was the smile on her face.

"If you're meant to be a mother, Charla, you will be. I hardly even know you, but I know that you deserve someone better than what you had."

I was about to ask a question I wasn't sure she'd answer. My curiosity wouldn't rest. There was a lot to learn about this woman, but something about her spoke to me and made me smile without words. She intrigued me and awakened something in me that had been dormant.

Despite my job and the amount of confidence it took to pull it off, I still wanted romance. I craved it. I wanted to belong to someone special. The guys gave me shit about being a hopeless romantic, but I didn't care. Charlene had unknowingly called to that part of me that believed in romance and true love, and I couldn't ignore the achingly strong pull she had on my senses.

"You said you guys had been together since you were nineteen. Are you married? Getting divorced?"

She let out a low, uncomfortable laugh.

"Oddly, I never bothered him about getting married. Did I want him to ask me? Of course I did. But, sometimes, it appeared my friends were more concerned than I was about it. They even questioned if it was me or him who shied away from marriage. I honestly couldn't give them an answer. Now that I'm no longer with him, it's occurred to me that neither of us seriously broached the subject. Humm," she said under her breath like the revelation was just now making an impact on the way she saw their relationship.

"We would mention it in passive conversation, like it was the changing weather, and then dismiss it. We were so used to being together that we were comfortable. Our behavior where marriage was concerned is something else that comes to light to confirm that our breakup was inevitable or maybe even long overdue. Maybe we were just passing the time until something better came along."

She shrugged as if knocking some of the ideas in her head away.

"What do *you* think?" I asked her. "I can tell that you're hurt by the breakup and about the way he handled things, but what do you believe? Could you have been unconsciously waiting until something better came along?"

Her brows lifted. "I don't know. I loved him. But it was never that all-consuming, I would die for you kind of love that old people are always talking about. I gave so much of myself to him that I think I lost sight of who I was. If he'd proposed and wanted to get married, I would have married him because it was the next logical step. The more I turn it over in my head, I think I'm more upset about how easily he was able to walk away after spending all those years together than over the actual breakup itself. It presents a hard-to-swallow perspective that I wasted all those years with the wrong person. And what's even harder to accept is that I believe I settled for him."

I bit into my bottom lip to suppress the smile threatening to surface. It pleased me that she was doing enough self-reflection to accept that maybe she had been with the wrong person all along.

"I know it's easier said than done, but you're going to have to release the past so you can build the future that you want." I couldn't help running a caring hand over her arm. "What do *you* want, Charla? That's what you have to focus on and figure out now."

I didn't expect us to go that deep, but I was comfortable talking to her. I had never had this level of conversation with a woman before, but I wasn't going to tell her that. She needed to talk, and I was honored that she was willing to trust me with her secrets.

"What about you? Tell me some of your secrets. Are you from Richmond? Have any family here?" she asked.

I swallowed hard, gathering myself.

"I grew up in Los Angeles. Mother died of a drug overdose when I was seven. Came up in the foster care system. Ran away when I was fourteen. Lived on the streets until I started dancing at eighteen. I met Trent, a perfect stranger at the time, who was visiting a friend of his in LA. We ended up at the same party, one I'd snuck into to get free food. We struck up a conversation about hard times and trying to make a living in California. He told me about him and his mother facing homelessness for some time and that he was from Richmond. I liked the sound of a smaller city because I believed it could offer someone like me the kind of hope that the mean streets of LA just didn't offer. Trent exchanged numbers with me and said if I was serious about getting out of LA to look him up."

Silence filled the space, and I glanced over to find her listening intently, her empathetic eyes glued to my face.

"I moved here and lived on Trent's couch for a few months until I was able to get a place of my own. Eventually, I started listening to some of the free advice that goes through the club scene. I started saving my money and thinking about a better future. I ended up finally going back to school and getting my GED. Eventually, dancing became a catalyst for my future versus allowing it to suck me into its dark grips like it did when I first started."

I tapered off after that. What did she think of me?

"You didn't have any family that could have kept you from living on the streets?"

"No. When I tried to ask my mother about my father or family, she'd go silent on me, like the mere thought of talking about him or them physically hurt. I never tried to look for them either, figured I was better off in the system or on my own."

She nodded, and we both went silent. Was I being too revealing and straightforward with her? I wanted to be up-front and honest about myself and prayed that she wouldn't judge me based on my past and accept who I was now.

When I drove past the sign informing that we were outside the complex of luxury condos her address had led us to, I wasn't surprised. Charla was a well-established career woman, so I expected her home would be a reflection of her hard work.

"Nice place," I complimented.

We sat at the entrance with my arm sticking out the window, waiting for her to decide whether or not she wanted to share the combination to the huge fancy metal gates protecting her community.

"Charla. I'm not a stalker. You don't have to worry about me creeping into your complex to do something stupid."

"126489," she mouthed. I punched the number in and waited for the gates to slide apart. I drove forward, noticing a guard station with two security personnel sitting inside.

Charla pointed me in the direction of her building when we came to a fork in the road. She reached into the small clutch purse that hung from her wrist like a keychain and extracted her keys.

We stopped in her driveway in front of her closed garage. The inside of this complex highlighted immaculate landscaping, and even the architecture of the building insinuated that the mortgage wasn't for the faint of heart.

Each building housed four condos, but they were built so each tenant could enjoy the privacy of their own fenced-off yard. I reached over and stopped Charla from opening her door.

"Please, let me."

Getting out and walking around to her side of the car, I cracked my knuckles and inhaled a few deep breaths to combat my twitching nerves. This was a first for me. I'd always been confident, especially when it came to women. But Charla wasn't any woman. She was beautiful, interesting, and although we just met, I cared about what she thought of me. I cared about making her feel better, even if I wasn't the one who caused her grief. I didn't even care if we had sex or not. I only knew I had to satisfy my strong desire to be near her.

Chapter Six

Ransome

We were here. I was about to walk into Charla's home. The idea struck me like a physical slap and sparked an unfamiliar unease. *She makes me nervous.* I couldn't grasp the concept, much less accept it, since I was often the one who rattled nerves.

She pushed the door open and stood in place for a second like she was having a final heart-to-heart in her head with the decision she was making. I didn't move or say a word, allowing her whatever time she needed to make the best choice for herself.

It was seconds, but it felt like hours before she stepped inside, flipped on her lights, and tossed her keys and wristlet on the door side table. Her condo was finely furnished. A large pale yellow couch sat as the living room's centerpiece, adorned with striped and colorful decorative throw pillows.

Two darker caramel-colored chairs sat a parallel distance away from the couch, separated by a wood and glass coffee table with a decorative accent atop it. One of the chairs had a furry cream throw thrown across the arm. The neat setup resembled an ad in a Better Homes Magazine.

The wood that made up the base of the coffee table matched the color of the chairs. The east and west walls gave the room privacy and were adorned by large hand-painted portraits. The south wall was all glass and opened to a deck and lighted pool in the distance. The snow-white area rug sat atop glossy hardwood floors, and splashes of red, gold, and green pieces throughout the space brought more life into the living room.

Charla's living space took me in as much as I took it in. When I glanced up into Charla's waiting gaze, the tension I managed to beat back returned with a vengeance that made me flex my neck and shoulders.

Framed photos of varying sizes depicting her and her friends sat atop a table that led into the dining area. I stepped closer to the display, interested in more aspects of Charla's life. In the background of one of the photos was the Eiffel Tower. Big Ben sat behind them in another, and her waving while walking the Great Wall was depicted in another.

This woman was accomplished and had lived. Was I out of my element with her? This was the first time I considered that someone was out of my league despite having dated a large variety of women, some much richer than Charla. Therefore, I believe my unease was attributed to something deeper than her living space or impressive social status.

"You can have a seat," she said, ushering her hand toward her couch. "Would you like something to drink?"

"Water, please," I replied while taking the seat.

Charla's eyes weren't as glossy as they'd been at the club, so her alcohol buzz had likely worn off a bit.

She returned, and I prayed she couldn't read the rare bout of intimidation rolling through me.

"Considering I've never had a one-night stand, how is this supposed to work? Do we just go for it?"

I choked down a gulp of water and gave my chest a hard thump with my palm to help clear my airway. Charla sat next to me, brushing my leg with her warm one. She unnerved me, and if she hadn't noticed it before, I'm sure she observed my current fumble. The only other time I recalled being this on edge was my first night on the stage. That night, I forced myself to face my fear and succeeded. "Come and sit on my lap," I commanded after leaning forward to place my water on the coffee table. A wide smile spread across Charla's lovely mouth before she scooted back on the couch. She pulled her legs up and repositioned herself into a kneeling position before climbing over my lap. She straddled me, taking our situation quickly from one extreme to the next.

Physically, she was warm perfection, but mentally, I couldn't stop a reel of ideas about us becoming a legit couple from consuming my mental focus. There were also clips of the nine hundred and ninety-nine different sexual positions I wanted to put her in swimming around in my head as well.

My heart pumped a mile a minute, the thump beating in my ears. Her dazzling smile charmed mine to the surface and help stabilize my mental focus. Her weight pressing into my thighs kept me hot, hard, and pulsing in places that had never pulsed before.

Dropping my gaze, I lingered on her lips a moment before tracing the beautiful line of her jaw. Every facial feature was admired until my eyes reunited with her lovely, big brown ones.

Captivated, I took my time admiring her, letting my eyes feast on the bend of her kissable lips. I swallowed hard, the lush sight making my mouth water for a taste of her lips, her mouth, her tongue. The warm fluidity of her skin, pebbling under my touch, emitted a radiant energy I eagerly absorbed.

Her eyes, larger than average, peered into the depths of mine, so deep I swore she could read my emotions, sense my intentions, and predict my future. She didn't just look at me. She stared right through my physical presence and saw the real *me*, the part everyone else ignored.

In the dim setting of the club, her eyes appeared black or even dark brown. With a bit of light shining on them, a cinnamon brown twinkled brightly with a rainbow of lighter brown flecks at the outer edges of her iris.

All I had to do was lean forward to capture those lush, naturally kiss-swollen lips, but I hesitated. My hands slid up her thighs, soft and supple, even covered by jeans. She was warm and smooth and smelled good, like cinnamon and warm honey.

I couldn't lure my eyes away from hers if my life depended on it. We hadn't even slept together, yet I felt a deeper physical connection to her than any other woman.

Her fingers slid teasingly up my arm, leaving goosebumps and a slight tingle in their aftermath. Anxious for our first kiss, my tongue licked across my bottom lip, mimicking the way Charla's slipped across hers. Her lust-heavy eyes relinquished the hold they had on mine and fell to my mouth.

She fidgeted, waiting for me to make a move. When she could take no more of my lingering need to soak her in, she leaned in and placed her lips against mine. The first warm touch was all it took to inspire me to seek out more. A few lingering pecks followed, allowing us to feel each other out.

Lust consumed me. It took control of my senses and my visionary desires were lost to my need to feel. I pressed harder, deepening the kiss to satisfy my hunger. I needed to explore her with more than my hands and mouth.

Circling her waist, I tugged her into me with a roughness I didn't intend but couldn't help. My eager tongue licked across her lips, enticing her to open for me before I dived in to satisfy my sense of taste.

My heart galloped in my chest, and the sensation of floating someplace above the clouds had my head all messed up. I'd never experienced this type of mind-blowing exhilaration with anyone. I never cared about anything other than achieving my goal of making a woman come so that I could get my turn.

When Charla's hot tongue licked across the top of mine, a searing pang of satisfaction had me moaning into her mouth. There was no way she didn't feel my erection, hard enough to start slicing through the material of my pants if I didn't do something about it soon. It had been four months since I had been with a woman, one who'd ended up being boring and unresponsive until she came.

"God, you taste good," I muttered between deep breaths. "So sweet."

Why were my damn hands shaking like my system was short-circuiting? Or maybe it was being re-wired to Charla's specifications.

She backed away a little, her stare intense like she'd picked up on the same all-consuming energy that had consumed me. Did she see the emotions in my eyes I didn't fully understand yet?

I leaned back in and feathered my mouth along her neck, not wanting her to notice my erratic and emotional reaction. My lips played along her neck and collarbone, caressing her soft, warm flesh and plying a tender portion between my lips. I licked up the warm column with deliberate torture, using my teeth to graze the tender flesh and loving her gasping reaction.

My fingers brushed the bottom of her silk top before I gripped and lifted it. She took one half of the top and helped me lift it over her head. Everything about this woman enticed me. Her scent. Her look. The way she offered her body to me. The way she kissed me like it would be our first and last time. Every layer of herself she revealed, physically or mentally, *did* something for me and stirred desires I wasn't aware existed.

Her syrupy brown skin was a feast for my eyes, the sight sending lust-ridden messages to my brain—the supple texture and its flawless surface capturing my attention. Her skin bore a gentle brown glow like she'd been polished and kissed with a pinch of gold glitter that made her sparkle.

I was naturally tanned and olive-complected, but often enhanced my natural color with more exposure to ultraviolet rays for a more dramatic effect on stage. Charla's darker skin against my considerably lighter tone provided a contrast that gave definition to the word erotic.

The contrast between our tones excited my senses, creating a whole new category of lust. We complemented each other, and the swirling tones fed more life into our desires that flared like a barely contained fire.

I had been with a few African-American women before, but our time together had been so fleeting I could hardly recall the experience. Charla was a woman I knew I'd never forget.

She was a buffet of seductive parts that would certainly tempt the most disciplined man. We didn't break our kiss when she began to lift my shirt. I simply shifted slightly to give her space to help me out of it. We reluctantly parted when my shirt was at my neck, and as soon as it was over my head, my lips were back on hers.

"Let's go," she suggested, breaking our kiss again.

Her eyes were so heavy—her alcohol high had been replaced with a lust high. Unable to help myself, I leaned in for another kiss and allowed my tongue to make one last twirl around hers.

She backed off my lap, leaving my dick heavy and aching with a need so strong that I groaned deep in my throat. I lifted my eyes and took her in fully, standing before me, looking like the unattainable woman of my dreams. Damn, she was sexy.

I slid to the edge of the couch when she took my hand. She tugged me along, leading me to her bedroom. When she let go of my hand and walked further into her bedroom, I eyeballed her nice round ass again.

It had taken everything in me at the club to keep my eyes off her ass when the lights came on. My hands sliding over that ass as she slid off, on, and over my dick a moment ago had put me in a trance. The anticipation of being with her had put me in a chokehold since the moment I laid eyes on her.

She stepped into her dim room and disappeared against the darkness, leaving only her steps behind. I stood at the door until the bedside lamp illuminated the space. She picked up a remote and pushed a few buttons that made music spill softly from someplace inside the room.

My brain was too muddled to even care about what music was playing and who was singing it. Charla owned my focus. My gaze soaked in her thin black lacy bra and zeroed in on the shadow of her nipples.

She reached behind her and unhooked her bra next, letting the front drop a teasing inch to flash me her cleavage before she dropped her arms and let it slide down until it hit the floor.

For a change, I had the opportunity to enjoy a performance. Her tits were full and perky, the tips hard and begging to be licked, sucked, and bitten. She lifted and sat her foot, still encased in a sexy stiletto, against the edge of the foot of the bed. The pose she presented without her bra would forever remain a portrait in my head.

She didn't have to call me over or instruct me. I was at her feet, undoing one of those sexy heels she wore and kissing her ankle while completing the task and switching to undo her other heel. Once I slipped the heels off, she stood before me, her eyes never breaking away from mine.

The little grin on her face was filled with promise and the kind of confidence that fueled my needs. When she reached down to undo her jeans, I stopped her.

"Please, let me," I insisted, unable to resist kissing each of her tempting nipples before proceeding with her pants. The gasp and little shiver she released at my lips on her puckered flesh only fed my desire, keeping it set on burning.

I wanted the honor of getting her out of the rest of those clothes. I undid her buttons and zipper and began the process of peeling her out of her jeans. I took my time about it, too, placing my fingers in the waistband before I proceeded to slide them down, enjoying the little wiggles of help she gave to assist me. More of her beautiful flesh met my gaze and stroked my desire with more need than I could handle.

Unable to stop myself, my hands skimmed, lingered, and squeezed her supple skin. Her lower stomach, right above her thin black silk panties, was like warm perfection against my lips. Ample thighs and sexy hips got their turn, satiny to the touch. I allowed my mouth the pleasure until the jeans were pooled at her feet.

I didn't remove the jeans from around her ankles right away. The need to take a gradual stroll back up her body consumed me. Her languid movements, the rise and fall of her chest, her legs rubbing together, her nails biting into my shoulder, spoke for how she begged to be satisfied.

On my way up, my fingers skimmed naked hot flesh, my palms were filled with sexy thighs, and my hands squeezed her firm round ass. It wasn't enough. My eyes feasted on the swell of her breast, her flat stomach, and finally, the panties that covered the area I was eager to sample.

Charla's body was in impeccable shape. You didn't get a body like this unless you invested time. The knowledge that she found time to invest in herself added weight to how impressed I was with her.

She was toned, and although her definition was visible, it didn't take away from her sex appeal. She mentioned she was turning twenty-nine, therefore it was officially her birthday since it was after two a.m. I planned to give her at least three gifts she would remember for years.

I pegged her for a younger woman, certainly younger than me, but who cared about age when our chemistry was off the charts? Whatever she and her friends were doing, concerning the youthful glow they possessed, they needed to bottle it and sell it.

Lifting her with ease, I sat her on the edge of the bed to finally pull her legs free of the jeans. My eager hands began a lingering exploration again, cupping her right ankle before taking a smooth ride up until my view aligned with those silky black panties and the delicate crease of her pussy print.

Once I discarded her jeans, sweeping them carelessly off to the side, I drew her up and back into my hold. Her hot skin against mine was a sensation so new and addicting I shivered.

Breathe, I reminded myself before slowing my frenzied caresses. I drew back to calm myself. My fingers teased her waistline before I flattened my hands and slid them up her body until I had her perfect tits cupped in my palms. One soft squeeze closed her eyes and drew out a low moan of approval from her that heightened my arousal.

I massaged her tits and leaned in to meet her halfway to another magnetic kiss. This one was gentle and meticulously slow. The swirl of our lips, of our tongues, produced a heat that burned so hot that I panted. The hot passion being drawn from within the depths of us made me believe we were flowing on the same charged wavelength.

With her pressed tightly against me, my hands automatically ran down her back until they were sliding over the curved expanse of her ass. The globes were lush clouds of soft flesh that required my complete attention. I squeezed before sliding my hands lower and lifting her.

When her legs wrapped around my waist, the sensual position felt right. I would have been done with any other woman by now. We would have gotten what we wanted from each other, and she or I would have been heading home.

Not this time. I wanted to savor Charla. If this would be our one time together, I wanted to remember it. More importantly, I wanted her to remember me. I shuffled around the foot of her bed to the side with her clinging to me. Our lips smacked while our tongues continued to explore. She broke the seal of our kiss.

"Condoms, top drawer, behind us," she said, blindly pointing.

Her lips were on my neck and chest as I turned, opened the drawer, and reached for what I saw was one of two boxes of new condoms. I gripped the box of magnums and inched us back until we bumped into the immaculately dressed king-sized bed.

I was reluctant to pause for even a second but did so when I lowered her to the bed. She shamelessly fucked me with her eyes while I admired her naked body laid out against the plush black silk comforter. She used her elbows to back further into the bed, allowing me room to climb in and position myself at her knees.

The lust-heavy smile she flashed showed off a perfect row of straight teeth that sank into her bottom lip. Charla had me so hypnotized it took me a moment to register her easing up closer to me. Her fingers worked the button loose and the zipper of my pants down until her thumbs were looped in the waistband.

She dragged the jeans down as far as my butt before she drew so close her breaths teased the skin on my stomach. Glancing up at me, she smirked before she finished her task. I helped by shoving my jeans the rest of the way down my legs and kicking them off my feet when they pooled at my ankles.

Charla backed further into the bed and invited me to join her with one flick of her freshly manicured finger. Desire peeked from the lustful glint in her eyes. She'd seen me damn near naked on stage, so she already knew what I had to offer.

"How do you want to do this?" she asked. The eagerness in her voice registered. Honestly, I assumed she would have chickened out by now, especially after having let slip that her ex, whatever his name was, may have been the only man she'd been with sexually.

"I wasn't lying at the club. You can do whatever you want," I told her, and meant it, too. My tongue slid across my lips in an attempt to stave off the eagerness rolling through me like charged electrons, but it didn't work.

The devilish smirk on her face widened, and a hint of mischief flashed in her lust-heavy eyes when they landed on the bulge in my green silk boxers. We were going to have a good time for the rest of the night and until morning. The idea was a prophecy in my head.

Chapter Seven

Charla

Was I about to have unapologetic sex with this sexy ass man I hardly knew? We shared a charged connection that drew me in so deeply that I never wanted the sensation to go away.

Glancing into his hypnotic eyes, tasting his lips and tongue—it was all too good to be true. His hands on me lured every drop of lust I possessed to the surface and left me with no choice but to explore further to see how high he could take me.

My eyes dropped to the big bulge in his boxers, imagining how something that large would stretch my walls and massage my pussy from the inside. We hadn't even gotten to the good stuff yet, and I already knew that this was a night I would never forget.

He'd given me permission to do whatever I wanted with him and reminded me that he wasn't kidding about the declaration. The way he said it and the tone in which he made the promise had my juices flowing like a freeway.

I directed him, tugging him by the arm.

"Sit here."

He complied, sitting with his back to the headboard. I hadn't paid as much attention to him as I assumed I had while he was on stage. Therefore, the intimidating bulge in his boxers as I edged closer had me excited and scared at the same time. I reached for his last stitch of clothing, anxious to introduce my eyes to the prize hidden behind the material.

He lifted and allowed me to slide the silky material down his toned legs, and I paused right before he popped out. Carter was the only man I'd been with, and although he was above average, Ransome's size, along with this situation, had me stressing at a time when my lust knocked.

Lust was having no part of the doubt I was allowing to creep into my head. It yelled, *"Bitch, fuck Carter! Sit on that big ass dick and have a fucking party!"*

Ransome must have noticed my temporary moment of reluctance. He offered a smirk laced with mischief before he ran the backs of his fingers up my arm.

"Don't worry. You'll be in control. You can take as much as you want," he assured me.

I shook my head before nodding with more confidence, attempting to rid myself of the last shreds of doubt as I continued my task of sliding his boxers down his body. My panties came down with a quick swipe in case the last bit of my alcoholic courage wore off and forced me to change my mind.

***

Ransome

Charla crawled to me and pressed a soft kiss on my lips before she took her position over my legs. I assisted, unable to keep my hands off the woman. One second without touching her was too long.

A moment ago, I noticed she hadn't hidden her surprise or reluctance at seeing my size. She also attempted but failed to hide her doubts about what we were about to do.

However, I noticed the sparks reigniting in her eyes. Some assumed dancers found ways to stuff their G-strings to make their dicks longer. A few did it for entertainment purposes, but not me. I considered myself lucky. My dick, along with my body, were the assets I possessed at a time when I had fallen into the endless pit of homelessness. And I wasn't sorry I'd had to use my body to feed, clothe, and keep a roof over my head.

Unfortunately, size didn't matter when it came to keeping a woman for the long haul. My job always drove the good ones away. It didn't stop me from trying, though.

I wanted Charla. *Bad.* Knew it the moment I saw her and more so when I talked to her.

Right now, she mesmerized me. Her ex was a distant memory that I hoped would disappear from her mind completely. She focused on me, giving me every bit of the kind of attention I lacked in my life.

She had me caught up in waves of lust and untamed emotions so strong that sparks of terror shot through me along with the rush of hot exhilaration. She was gorgeous in clothes, but she was a mystical goddess in the nude.

Charla was the kind of woman you took your time and admired. The warm glide of my hand over her sensuous body, the citrus and natural flavor she produced left me salivating for more, and the visual stimulation of her smooth skin and her luscious curves gave me a natural high. The emotions she'd unknowingly coaxed to life kept stirring within me and were a whole other matter I couldn't accurately describe in words.

My anxious fingers went straight between her splayed legs and slid right into place.

"Your pussy is dripping wet for me, baby. And so fucking hot."

I whispered my lust-riddled words against her neck before sending a long stroke of my tongue along the thin vein that ran up the side. The tip of my tongue caressed the bottom of her lobe.

"You're doing this to me, making me so fucking hot for you," she whispered, finding my lips again before sending her tongue across them. I used the opportunity to explore her mouth, tasting remnants of the alcohol she consumed along with a flavor that was uniquely addicting and all her.

I couldn't wait to get my mouth on her pussy. She was currently using it expertly to tease me. The heat between her legs radiated into me, giving me a hint of the warm, wet massage waiting for my aching dick.

Her round tits filled my hands perfectly while her raisin-hard nipples flirted with my fingertips. Her supple hips, her ample ass, and the silky canvas of her skin all worked in tandem to lure me deeper into her realm.

My dick could put a wrought iron spike to shame. The level of my overcharged desires was a testament to her seductive powers over me. Powers she didn't even know she possessed.

When I drew her body into mine with a quick, hard jerk, her hot pulsing pussy smashed against my throbbing dick.

"Shit!"

The curse word burst from us simultaneously while I fought the desperate urge to thrust into her.

She kissed me with the passion of a long-time lover, exploring my mouth and savoring each kiss like she was starved for it.

I gladly fed her my tongue while exploring the velvety contours of hers. She broke the kiss and traced my jaw with her soft lips. Her thighs squeezed against me, adding to the sweet torture of anticipation that drove me crazy.

"Charla," I pushed out her name, breathless. The smirk she flashed let me know that she knew she was driving me mad. Her quick breaths hit my face while her lips tickled my ear.

"I can't wait to see if I can take it all," she whispered, allowing her lips to scrape the edges of my lobe.

Her hot words made my dick jump and intensified the needy ache racing through me. I had to have her now, or I would burst from the anticipation alone.

Chapter Eight

Charla

At first, Ransome's size gave me pause, but I changed my mind when we continued to explore each other. Now, all I could think about was getting as much of him into me as my body would allow. I reached over and picked up the box of condoms I had bought weeks ago.

In my head, the condoms were a physical representation of my quest to move on with my life. Ransome tracked every move I made, his breathing quick, sharp. The anticipation in his gaze and the way his tongue traced his lips encouraged me to move faster.

After I ripped the box open, I tore off a condom and reached for his dick. My hand wrapped around a silk-covered hot iron.

Stroking up and down his length had me holding in my sighs. Seeing clear hot precum seeping from the tip of his thick pole had my taste buds watering for a sample and my pussy juices leaking in anticipation.

Fuck it!

I was ready to fuck, but I had to have a taste of this man right now. Instead of sliding the condom over his dick, I delighted in the way he looked in my hands. Smiling, I was breathing hard like we were already having sex. I leaned in and kissed the tip, making the pearl of cum I'd spotted stretch between my lips and his dick.

My tongue swiped across my lips, tasting the salty-sweet mix that instantly made me smile. I licked him again, once, twice, and on the third time, I pushed him past my lips and let him fill my mouth until the head touched my throat. My mouth watered around this length.

The man's dick was like sweet nectar to a woman starved of these decadent desires for way too long. I feasted on Ransome's dick, licking, sucking, and doing my best to jam him down my throat. I didn't notice how into the act I was until his words drew me out of my determined haze.

"Baby, you're going to make me come. I'm not ready yet."

I eased up off his dick, continuing to give light strokes with my hands wrapped around it. I was almost afraid to let go for fear I would wake up, and this would all have been a vivid dick dream.

"Her turn," he said eagerly, licking his lips and staring down at my pussy. The man lifted and tossed me down on the mattress so fast, I didn't even have time to be shocked. By the time I caught my bearings and glanced up, he was kneeling before my closed legs with his strong hands on either side of my knees, keeping them closed.

"I want you to part these sexy legs, but do it slowly, very slowly."

Like an obedient child, I nodded. The sexy timbre of his tone had me ready to do whatever he asked. He dropped his hands, and I spread my legs gently while watching him watch me.

His eyes overflowed with lust before widening when my pussy lips began to part. The view of him licking his lips and breathing hard like the act alone was getting him off had me shamelessly leaking all over my silk comforter.

The wider I spread my legs, the closer he drew into me. First, his warm breath washed over the insides of my thighs, then higher until it breezed over my wet pussy lips, cooling them.

The simple act of watching him being drawn in by my little show had me about to burst. In a flash, his mouth was on me. His tongue edged across my wet lips in one long, firm stroke that made my whole body quake.

"Damn!" I moaned out the word, biting into my lip and stretching my neck to see him work.

"Mmm," he moaned and continued to do so while circling my hungry hole. He dipped his tongue inside me and slurped to make sure he didn't miss out on any of my juices. His hot tongue licked the ache thundering through my core, his stroke dulling the irritating throb and filling me with tingling pleasure.

His tongue waved along my wet lips before he let the tip kiss my clit. When he squeezed my clit between his lips and sent his tongue chasing after it, I rotated my hips and thrust at his face. I moaned so loud it sounded like I was possessed, my voice traveling from another dimension.

He positioned his finger before sliding it in and out of me along with his hot tongue, spreading wet joy all over and through my lady parts. His moans added to the erotic trance and had my bottom lifting off the bed to follow his tongue when he backed away to reposition for a better angle.

Thankfully, he didn't tease me. He went right back in, lapping up my juices. He was licking my pussy too damn good and teasing the edges of my inner walls with long tongue strokes that drew passion from every pore.

"Ran. Oh. Ran. Some," I cried, doing my best to fuck his face. The man was murdering my clit and devouring my core with such masterful precision I doubted it had been a hot minute, and I was already screaming for him to have mercy on me.

"Shit," I called, sketching the word out so long it got caught in my throat. The orgasm hit, erupting in my core before sending the rush of the spectacular high through my quivering body.

"Oh my. Go-o—Mmm." Who the hell knew what I was saying. I damn sure didn't because I was floating on pure, unfiltered bliss.

It took me a while to drift back to reality. It had been nearly six months since my last orgasm, and the one I just enjoyed was one of the strongest I had experienced. I sat up, and the sight of Ransome's hard dick had me patting the bed for the condom I had forgotten about. Too eager to get the next phase of our session going, I gave up my search for the lost condom and reached for another.

Clenching the condom wrapper between my teeth, I ripped it open before slipping it out of the package. Thankfully, my fantasy of meeting a big-dick-pussy-slayer had prompted me to purchase multiple condom sizes.

I admired the extraordinary sight of Ransome's pulse thumping through the head of his beautiful dark-pink dick before I made a circle with my thumb and forefinger and slid the condom down.

Damn!

The sight of my fingers not closing around the circumference of him had me squeezing my thighs together. He was going to wreck my pussy, and I wasn't going to do shit but let him accomplish the mission.

I shifted my position, lifting high on my knees, and angled myself above his dick, anticipating the moment when he would impale me. The excitement rolling through me added to the way his thumb circled my erect nipple.

Hot and hard, I released a strangled gasp laced with satisfaction when the first few inches split my lower lips and pulsed into me. Ransome's eyes slammed shut when I eased up an inch and came down with enough force to push him in deeper.

His fingers dug into the flesh of my waist but didn't interrupt my slow descent. I relaxed my pelvic muscles and bared down harder to inch more of him inside me. His thick girth put a stretching pressure against my walls and had me shaking.

My God!

***

Ransome

Charla worked my dick into her overwhelmingly tight and very wet pussy. She didn't rush the process either. Sheer torture mixed with heart-pulsing pleasure thundered through me at her purposeful movements. Slow, sensual movements eased me into her until she was working me in and out with her movements alone. The sight kept me riveted to her body and her eyes when she lifted them to watch me watch us.

Halfway in, I was reduced to releasing low hisses and moans to stave off the hot pangs of lust that were already inspiring me to come. It was too soon. My desire to please Charla for as long as possible and me slamming my eyes shut was all that beat back the urge.

"Don't stop," I begged between clenched teeth after regaining a little of my composure. I hadn't been able to open my eyes yet. The sight of Charla easing down on my dick would surely make me lose it.

When I was most of the way inside her, the slow rhythm of her rotation snatched my breath and began the process of stretching her walls to accommodate me. Her hot juices coated my dick and made it feel like I wasn't wearing a condom. I surrendered to her seductive movements, letting my eyes roll to the back of my head.

Her warm luscious lips found and covered mine. Hot and sweet all at the same time, I gladly accepted her kisses. The undoubtedly addictive shit she was doing to the lower half of me had me one breath from passing out.

Her pussy was casting a spell over my dick, marking it, possessing it, treating it to a gift so magnificent, I drowned in the juicy flow of every twist and turn.

I was accustomed to being in charge, setting the pace, and picking the position. Women didn't care as long as we fucked. Charla was the first woman I wanted to take sexual control, so she could seek out and indulge in her every whim and fantasy. However, she was unwittingly playing a role in fulfilling a fantasy I never saw coming.

The first glimpse I'd gotten of Charla at the club had captured my full attention, but now that I was here and in her bed, she hypnotized me further, branding me to never want any other woman.

The fuck? What am I saying...thinking?

Chapter Nine

Charla

Ransome had me on a new sexual level that I didn't know existed. I'd had good sex before, or at least I believed I had. Now, he had me doubting I even knew what good was.

His dick was down there, releasing waves of pure pleasure so strong I wanted to cry. My walls were stretched to the max, making the pleasure-ache radiate through my stomach and back.

"So…"

Forming a complete sentence was out of the question. How could I possibly think straight enough to speak when all I was capable of doing was complimenting him with my physical responses?

"Good," finally came out with a moan into his ear.

"You too," he gritted out before a low hiss helped him push out a long-winded, "Shit!"

I rocked and switched to rotating in tight circles, the weight of his dick not leaving anything untouched. Each movement gave me a different high and left me unable to decide which I liked better, this slippery, stretching pressure or the wet intensity of the pounding friction.

When he added his upward thrust, I decided that his participation drove all of the sensations home. He made me wet enough to drown his dick.

How was I not supposed to want *this* again? It had taken minutes to get to this point, and Ransome had me so open and hungry for him that I managed to get every inch of his thickness inside me. I ground into his upward thrust, so engrossed in the sensual act that I was dripping all over his balls.

Sensations I never knew existed were stroked by his long, solid thrust, some I believe he was inventing while going to a place that no man had gone before. *Carter who?* Not only was this sex good, but our emotions synced like we were well-acquainted lovers.

"That's it, baby. Take my dick. Make it yours."

"Holy fuck," I gritted out.

Ransome's encouraging words almost took me down. The way he admired me and encouraged my movements kept me motivated and so fucking turned on that he was inside me balls deep. I took it all, feeding a newly discovered, untamed desire.

I had no idea I could take that much dick. The stimulation was like experiencing a living sexual dream. I was finally getting personally acquainted with the phrase, wide-open, because this man had me throwing my pussy at him.

Muscles about to snap, head thrown back, eyes clamped shut, I gave this ride my all. I forced that man's dick so far up my pussy, I was left with no choice but to ride the sharp edges of pain while I overdosed on the intense waves of pleasure. The two forces met and snatched at my soul.

The dreaded ex rarely gave up control, so being able to be in charge of how I wanted the dick was liberating, and Ransome didn't mind it one bit. He told me that I could do whatever I wanted with him and kept his word.

I panted and gasped, riding him hard and fast before, I decreased my pace and allowed the flow of our movements to seep into the deepest depths of my being. And boy-o-boy, was it magnificent.

"So."

"Fucking."

"Good."

Each word synced with a hip rotation that left my walls clenching tighter around him.

***

Ransome

I literally fell into another world, the all-consuming one called Charla. There wasn't a thing she could have done that I didn't enjoy. The way her pussy clenched around my dick with such raw possession, like it was expressing through the wet spine-tingling movements that my dick belonged to her.

The way she owned me with every turn of her hips, with every passion-laced kiss, and with every seductively whispered word in my ear. She knew what to do to bring me and herself the greatest amount of pleasure. She worked my dick, turning on it, grinding on it, sliding up and down and bouncing on it.

"That's it, baby. Fuck me. Fuck, it's good," I whispered before flicking my tongue across one of her nipples and drawing it into my mouth.

It was like she was tuned into the movements, pace, and depth that gave me the greatest high and executed it. She was fucking me so well I was on the verge of exploding. She was so wet and tight down there that I questioned again if we'd even put the condom on.

"Charla, baby...."

"I know, me too," she answered, knowing what I was getting at without me having to finish my statement. She threw her arms around my neck in a way that she could cup the back of my head, splaying her fingers into the top of my hair as I hissed and moaned into her warm, sweet-smelling shoulder.

She pulsed against my dick, coming with me planted so deep inside her, I exploded too. My eyes rolled to the back of my head and remained there. An insane amount of pleasure controlled me. I could hear my voice repeating all types of foul words and language, but the volume of it was off in the distance, like I wasn't on the same plane as the sounds.

"Ransome, you're making me come." Charla screamed her release into my neck. I squeezed her body to mine while she continued to ride out our pleasure. Our movements stretched the pleasure out to one of the most exhilarating experiences of my life. I think she came a second time, but I was too out of it to know for sure.

Euphoria flowed in waves, taking me by force. I had never come so hard and long in my life. Not only did I experience a body orgasm, but I believe my mind exploded along with it.

Charla went slack against me even as she heaved to get oxygen into her lungs. We remained in each other's embrace until our heartbeats synced into a flowing rhythm.

***

Charla

When I finally caught my breath, I eased back to get away from Ransome's addictive body. Was it bad of me to want to go again already? Ransome's dick had gone down enough that the pressure on my walls had eased, but with his size, there was more than enough to still get me off.

His tight grip didn't loosen at my attempt to get away. I was experiencing that odd feeling you get once the fire dies down. I accepted that I didn't mind the feeling since I hadn't experienced any real emotions in years.

"Don't put me out yet. Can I take a quick nap first?" he whispered the question against my neck.

An instant smile surfaced at Ransome's quick words. He was worried that I was getting ready to put him out of my place. He blew a breath through his smile once he saw mine.

"Sure. You can stay. I'll grab a towel so we can clean up."

He released me from his tight hold, and I inched back. We groaned when his semi-erect dick slid out of me.

While I was in the bathroom, I gave myself a good wipe down. I plucked a fresh towel from my wardrobe and got it good, warm, and soapy for Ransome. On the short walk back, it had just occurred that I hadn't used condoms in so long it was weird knowing I was about to dispose of one.

After sitting on the edge of the bed next to him, I brushed his hand aside when he reached for the towel. I wanted to stroke him again, even if it was to clean him up.

I spread the towel over my hand and gripped the bottom of his shaft to slide the condom off. Once I had it off, I folded the towel around it and used the clean side to wash him again. He smiled the whole time, his intriguing expression indicating that he was fascinated by what I was doing to him.

Once that was done, I tugged the covers up his legs but left his beautiful dick in my view. On my walk back to the bathroom to flush the condom, I could feel his eyes on my naked body, and I loved it. I sensed that Ransome wanted me again like I wanted him, and I wasn't disappointed that he'd asked to stay for a *nap*. Nap, my ass, we were fucking again.

When I returned from the bathroom, the covers were up to his waist, and he was lying in my bed like he belonged there. He scooted to the middle and lifted the covers up in a gesture for me to climb in front of him.

For reasons I couldn't yet wrap my head around, I couldn't stop comparing this night to my ten-year relationship. In the past, the ex would lie back and start snoring almost immediately after sex. He didn't give a damn about getting clean. He damn sure didn't care about cuddling.

I climbed into my bed and scooted back until Ransome wrapped his arms around my waist and tucked me into his strong body. The flesh-on-flesh contact was refreshingly warm, invigorating, and surprisingly calming.

Ransome drew me into him so tight and snugly that my eyes fell closed at the comforting warmth that enveloped me. His soft lips pressed into my nape and made the hairs on my neck stand.

"Good night, Charla."

"Good night," I whispered back to him.

The warm flow of his steady breaths eased the last bit of tension from my aching muscles. My lips twitched a few times before a smile emerged. Then, something hit me.

Good night?

He'd asked to take a nap, not spend the night. His deceptive wordplay had won him more time with me. It won me more time with him, too. I would have been too ashamed to ask him to stay, too afraid that all he would see was desperation.

It felt damned good to be snuggled up with him like this. A low and contented sigh escaped before I allowed myself to drift into a peaceful oblivion.

Chapter Ten

Charla

When I peeled my eyes open, it only took a second for the warm press of Ransome's strong body against mine to register. His arms were wrapped around me like he was afraid I would sneak away from him in the middle of the night.

The sun peeked high in the sky, indicating that I was waking up later than usual. The blue digital numbers on my clock confirmed the sun's position, flashing 11:16. Ransome and I had slept for seven hours.

Damn!

Unless I was sick, I rarely slept past eight o'clock. I attempted to wiggle my way out of his embrace without him noticing, but his groggy voice and warm breath bathed my ear.

"Good morning," he said before squeezing his arms around me and closing me in tighter.

"Morning," I returned, trying to pretend like I didn't like him holding me so snug and tight. I was supposed to be finding a way to tell him that it was time for him to leave, not enjoying the way his strong arms felt around me, how his naked body felt pressed into mine, or enjoying the last remnants of his cologne mixed with his masculine scent.

I needed to be alone to prepare myself for never seeing him again. How the hell was I supposed to do that? How did anyone after a one-night romance?

"How about I make you breakfast before you go?" I volunteered. "Just because we won't be seeing each other again after today doesn't give me an excuse to be a bad host."

Why the hell did I just volunteer more of my time to Ransome? So much for following my first mind. This new section of my brain, the impulsive self-assured area, was apparently running things now.

A sweet kiss was placed against the back of my neck, and the long, dragging sniff of appreciation he took against my tender skin left the area pricked with goosebumps. Ransome wasn't stingy with his affections. I hadn't been savored in this way in so long, I'd forgotten how it felt to be desired.

Something large and hard pressed into my ass cheek. The erotic touch had me rubbing my legs against each other to fight the ache erupting in my lady parts.

Ransome pressed his lips to my neck again before dragging them along my skin until his mouth was at my ear.

"Can I have some more of that silky, wet, tight, gripping, sucking, and intoxicatingly sweet pussy? As you can feel, I can't help myself."

The answer was always going to be yes if he asked me like that.

Shit.

He pressed his erection harder against my ass to drive home his question and statement. I was supposed to be saying no, but my squirming body answered before I whispered, "Yes."

I cleared my throat, "Let me pee first."

Since it felt like grass had grown on my tongue, I also wanted to at least swish some mouthwash around in my mouth. I had slept so well cozied up to Ransome that I noticed a few drops of drool on my pillow and had likely been snoring like a worn-out dog.

My hair was a mess of tangles and strays. Somewhere in our affair last night, I lost the band I had around my ponytail, which gave my hair the freedom to do as it pleased. Thankfully, my fresh perm meant a few strokes of my fingers were enough to tame it.

A long sigh closed my eyes, and as soon as I sat on the toilet, sweet relief swept through me. All that alcohol I consumed last night was choosing now to come out. A steady stream, going strong for at least a minute, came to an abrupt halt when Ransome walked into my bathroom while I was on the toilet.

What the...?

My mouth dropped open, and I cupped my hand in front of my exposed lady parts, although Ransome had gotten a good look at the area last night.

He didn't comment, but the smile on his face indicated that he was aware that he had surprised me. He stepped up to my counter like he lived here, and began inspecting my toothpaste and mouthwash. Once he was satisfied with his choice, he poured himself a cap full of mouthwash and tossed it into his mouth.

My pee began to flow again when he threw his head up and gurgled the mouthwash, but the tension in my face hadn't eased up. He had slipped his boxers back on, but it didn't stop me from wanting to get another peek at what he covered.

Thinking about last night made every bit of stress on my face soften. Had I imagined the size of it, or had my tipsy mind and greedy body conjured up an image of my fantasy dick?

Ransome spat out the mouthwash and proceeded to splash water on his face. The bathroom was alive with uncertainty about us occupying the same space that was usually reserved for one's privacy—mine.

Thank god I didn't have gas. How embarrassing would that have been, I thought, wiping and side-eyeing him to make sure he wasn't looking.

When I stood, he backed away from the sink to allow me my turn to wash my hands and freshen up. He raised the toilet seat, and the sound of him peeing made me go still.

"You're awfully comfortable," I commented, taken aback by his behavior.

"Just with you. You're just so..." He paused and glanced up, his head tilted slightly, still peeing. "I don't know. There is something about you that makes me feel like I can just...be."

My brows lifted high at the statement, unsure how to take it. I should have walked out, but something, curiosity maybe, made me stay. I had never even seen Carter peeing.

Ransome's actions had me gawking at just how perfectly at home he was around me and in my space. What kind of energy was I giving off that made him this damn comfortable?

My gaze dropped low, and even though he was soft, his dick managed to show off that it was big and thick without the extra blood pressure. I stared long enough for him to glance up and catch me.

I didn't know this man, yet we were peeing in front of each other. I proceeded to brush my teeth, wash my face and give my pussy a quick wipe down, turning away from him to give myself a little privacy. A wide smile brightened my face when he flush, put the toilet seat back down, and proceeded to wash his hands. This man was trained, by who, I didn't care, but appreciated it.

If we were having sex again, no way was I about to say no or offer him dirty privates.

After washing his hands he gave some attention to his dick, wiping it thoroughly with a wet soapy towel. The craziest part of the situation was that I didn't even leave when I was finished, but continued watching him.

I stepped back into the bedroom with him trailing me. There was no reason to beat around the bush, so if we were doing this, we needed to get on with it. I stepped over to my nightstand, opened the drawer, and tore off a condom.

Ransome was at my back with his warm hands sliding around my waist. The boxers were gone, so the hard press of his dick into my back made me bite into my bottom lip.

His warm lips caressed my shoulder as he reached around and took the condom. He nudged me toward my highboy dresser. With my back to him, he placed my hands, spread apart, on top of the dresser. The wide mirror reflected our actions back to us. My stance automatically widened when he used the top of his hard body to bend me over the dresser.

His big hands palmed my tits first before he squeezed them with enough firmness to heighten my arousal. He used his teeth and freed up a hand to rip the condom open.

I waited, eyeing him anxiously in the mirror as he slipped it on with his eyes on me the whole time. His hardness rubbed against my backside while he completed the action.

I couldn't help but be enticed, ready, and willing. My back dipped, and my shoulders reared back, the movement lifting my ass to him. His hand slid around my waist before he reached down, adjusted, and thrust against my butt, like it was a final warning to back out before it was too late.

The head slid teasingly down the crack of my ass and kissed the underside of my cheeks. Hot and hard, his dick finally rubbed against my wet lips. I was ready the moment he pressed against my leaking wet folds, so it took concentrated effort to control my urge to push back against him.

Ransome's eyes remained locked on mine while I impatiently awaited the moment of our reconnection. When he shoved himself into me, harsh, lung-aching breaths blew out so fast and hard it made my chest burn. My heavy eyes dipped, but I wouldn't let them close. I wanted to see his reaction as badly as he appeared to want to see mine.

When he pulled back and surged forward to sink more of that delicious dick into me, my body liquified, and my knees wobbled. I choked down the gasps I needed to help me through the rush of pulsing sensations that raced through me.

His arm sat snug across my chest, helping to support me while he multitasked, teasing my nipple with his thumb. My weak knees were useless, so he, along with the dresser, supported my weight.

He backed out a third time and thrust into me harder and so much deeper that my head fell forward. My splayed fingers curled, scraping my freshly manicured acrylic nails against the varnished wood of my dresser.

Each thrust spread pleasure into my core, which was getting wetter by the second. Each thrust shook the dresser, making our pleasure-filled reflections dance. Each thrust made my cries, throaty moans, and desperate gasps grow louder as I fought to keep my eyes on Ransome's in the mirror.

His eyes remained on me even as he bit into my shoulder to keep his composure. He was fighting his own battle. I noticed the edgy twinge of desperation hidden within the depths of his lust-heavy eyes.

One of my hands sat splayed on the shiny wood of the dresser, and my other gripped the edge of the wood so hard, my knuckles threatened to break through the back of my hand.

Ransome's grip tightened, squeezing my waist and hip while pumping into me harder. His harsh breaths escaped more frequently, feeding into our lust-induced episode. The sex was as good as I remembered. The alcohol I consumed last night hadn't dulled anything.

"Let's move to the bed," he suggested, easing out of me and viewing the action with rapt interest. Could he tell that I'd been on the verge of coming?

After sitting on the bed, I scooted back and into the center.

"How do you want me?" I asked while he climbed in and placed his hands on my knees.

"Baby, stay right here and open these sexy ass legs."

After swallowing the big lump of lust his words put in my throat, my legs fell apart. It didn't take but a second for Ransome to position himself, aim, and thrust his way home.

One hard, long stroke was all it took to completely undo me. A series of throat-tickling moans flew out of my mouth and livened up my bedroom.

My legs were already spread wide, but Ransome placed one of his hands behind the bend of my knee and sent my leg upward, opening me to him. The position allowed him to slide even deeper. At this depth, I was all gasps and moans, and nothing intelligible flowed into my brain. My nails dug deep into his back and shoulder and clawed deeper into his skin with each thrust he delivered.

He placed his mouth against mine, swallowing my loud moans, kissing me, and devouring my tongue with the same intensity with which he fucked me.

The only words I knew at this point were, "Ransome!" And. "Oh my God!"

"Don't let this be the only time, Charla. Tell me it won't be our only time."

He pushed out the demanding words right when he had me on the verge of losing my damn sanity. It wasn't fair. I would have said anything he wanted to hear at this point.

"It...won't...be...the...last...time,' I heard myself choking out each word between sharp breaths.

"Promise me, Charla," he commanded. His words were as sharp as mine.

"I promise. Oh God, I promise!"

The promise was shouted out just as my mind threatened to split apart, and the rest of me hummed with unbelievable exhilaration. The building intensity of my passion scared the hell out of me, making me believe it would rip me apart. My greatest fear was once I came apart for Ransome, I wouldn't be put back together the same.

Nothing could be done to save me at this point. Ransome was overwriting my sexual resume. It was always difficult for me to orgasm at the bottom because the ex would go so fast, he'd miss all of the spots that mattered. As a result, I often faked it, pretending to come when he came.

"I'm about to…" The three words were as far as I got before I shattered into bliss-filled pieces. My heavy eyes slammed shut, my lids trembling from the tight squeeze. I reveled in the body-tingling, pulse-pounding beats of pleasure that erupted in my center and mercifully spread to every part of me.

Ransome's loud cries mingled with my words, some unintelligible and meant as compliments, telling him something about how good he fucked me and how good he made me come.

All I could think now that my mind had knitted itself back together was that I'd just had a hit of the most addictive drug on the planet. How the hell was I supposed to ever say no when all I wanted was a prescription with unlimited refills?

Chapter Eleven

Ransome

Trouble.

I was in so much trouble, I couldn't see a way to get myself out of it. And it wasn't just regular trouble either. I was in the kind of trouble that took sound decision-making, time, and planning to straighten out.

Charla was in my system, flowing through my blood and supplying me a new perspective on life—with her.

She kept her word, and after a round of the best sex I ever had in my life, she showered, slipped into a sleep shirt and sexy boy shorts, and went into the kitchen to start preparing our breakfast.

After a quick shower, I slipped on my boxers and wrinkled jeans. We had slipped back into a comfortable nap after our late-morning sex session. It was now after one, and I was no closer to being ready to leave as I was when I arrived last night.

It wasn't until I saw it crumpled in her living room near the coffee table that I noticed it was where I had left my shirt. A smile immediately surfaced at the sight of Charla in her kitchen, mixing something in a bowl. In that thin shirt with no bra and those tiny little shorts that showed off those long, toned legs, she claimed my attention as soon as I stepped into the room.

"Can I help?" I asked her, my feet tapping lightly along her hardwood floors on my way to join her in the kitchen.

She didn't hide the pensive expression at my question.

"You want to help? Can you cook? Better yet, *what* can you cook?"

I shrugged. "Lots of stuff. You do the eggs and…" I paused, checking out the package before continuing. "…the vegan sausages. And I'll make the pancakes since you already have the batter mixed."

"Okay," she answered, the smile on her face wide. The sight of her joy fulfilled some need within me I wasn't aware existed.

Oddly, I was at home standing next to Charla at her stove. She scrambled the eggs and turned the sausages as I flipped our pancakes. Who knew the morning after could be fun? Who knew cooking with a woman could actually create joy?

I wasn't a full-blown vegetarian, but I rarely ate meat besides seafood. A glimpse in Charla's refrigerator showed it was stocked with a variety of vegan and plant-based foods. The shrimp and fish I spotted let me know that, like me, she wasn't a full vegan or vegetarian either.

She'd expressed surprise at my offer to help her cook a moment ago, therefore, I believe my actions were impressing her. I prayed I intrigued her enough to want to see me again. She said that our sex wouldn't be the last time, but I hadn't been playing fair when I'd asked.

She was unaware of the strength of the pull she had on me. It had to be unnatural. It couldn't have been normal to desire someone you hardly knew so strongly that you didn't recognize yourself. I hadn't even known her for twenty-four hours, yet the tugging in my belly wouldn't let up. Although I couldn't reconcile it in my head, there was a sense of knowing in my soul that also revealed itself.

I flipped the last pancake while Charla set out our plates, glasses, and the container of orange juice on the table. She frowned at her phone sitting on the table, ringing and vibrating. It had beeped a couple of times when we were in her bedroom—no doubt her friends checking on her. She reached and picked it up before turning her back.

"Hey, girl. What's up?"

Her tone was low, but curiosity sharpened my hearing enough to understand every word.

"Don't you 'hey-girl-what's-up' me. What's up with you? Why the hell haven't you called us yet?"

Her friend was loud enough on the other end that I made out her words.

"I'm sorry, but...."

She glanced back and caught me smirking.

"I'm still here," I yelled toward her phone, completing her sentence.

Charla's priceless expression conveyed shock and hints of joy.

Her friend's voices carried louder, lighting up the phone line. Their words were fast and jumbled. Were they fussing or giving her words of encouragement?

"I'll call you guys later," she mumbled into the phone before clicking it off and setting it on the table.

"Ice?" she asked, doing her best to keep her lips from turning into a smile while pouring a glass of orange juice. I shook my head at her question, knowing ice was the furthest thing from her mind. She pointed at something else, skirting the subject of us.

"I don't often drink coffee, but I can make some if you'd like," she said, still not commenting on her short phone conversation or my interruption.

"No to the coffee," I answered, smiling at her. The little smile tugging at the corners of her sexy lips let me know that she was okay.

I turned off the stove, sat the spatula in the sink, and me and the stack of four medium-sized pancakes joined Charla at the table. This was new territory for me. I never stuck around a woman's place long enough to eat with her.

If I didn't think it was too weird, I would pack a bag and spend the remainder of the weekend with Charla. I liked her. A lot. Being around her was easy, natural, and simply enjoyable.

How could any man be stupid enough to leave a woman like her? Was she hiding a nasty habit? Did she have mental problems?

I stopped flipping through the Rolodex of possible reasons when I remembered her saying she tried with her ex and was unable to have a baby. Children or no children were a dealbreaker for a lot of people. However, I couldn't see leaving a woman like Charla for any reason when there were so many options to be explored.

"You're not what I expected, Ransome. I thought dancers were all about hitting it and quitting it."

I mulled over my words before replying. What did she see in me that made her make that statement?

"Some of us are that way, but some of us honestly want some normalcy outside of work. I started dancing because I had two choices: dance or starve. As I mentioned briefly last night, I made a game plan when I finally woke up, grew up, and listened to the older dancers when they gave money and investment advice."

"What sort of game plan?"

I mentioned some of my goals to her last night, but she may have been too tipsy to recall anything I said. She forked a helping of eggs into her mouth and awaited my response.

"Some guys live under the guise that they can dance forever. They aren't willing to accept that eventually you age out or you can get hurt. Any number of things can happen. It took me a couple of years to wise up, but when I did, I invested in things that would earn me a living when dancing is no longer an option."

She leaned closer, and her eyebrows lifted in interest.

"I was fortunate to have the skill set of cutting hair, a skill I picked up when I was homeless in California. I cleaned up at a shop for a few dollars, along with learning how to cut hair and groom. The lessons turned out to be way more valuable than the money. And using social media for advertising and to show off my skills has also been a blessing. The first thing I invested in when I saved enough from dancing was my barber shop. And not an old shop someone was looking to get rid of either. I purchased the land and building. There are small apartments on the top levels of the building that I'm leasing as well. "

Her smile widened at the confession. I believed pride was what I saw flash in her eyes.

"Wow, that's amazing. Are you still buying or have you already purchased it?"

"I've bought it. With the money I make from dancing, it only took me a few years to pay it off. Monday through Wednesday or whenever I am not dancing, I'm there, cutting, edging, shaving, and grooming men."

Her gleaming smile enticed mine to make an appearance.

"I'm impressed," she said. "You're not at all what I assumed. As a matter of fact, you seemed to be the opposite of what I assumed. Therefore, let me apologize to you for assuming when I should know better than to judge a book by its cover or, in your case, a man by his job."

Her words had me beaming with a level of contentment I never experienced before. She eyed me for a long moment before asking another question.

"Do you have any other types of investments?"

"I started investing into a retirement account before the barbershop. After I finished paying off the barbershop, I started investing in a home."

Charla stopped eating completely. She placed her chin in her palm and stared with a prideful expression on her face. I couldn't contain my smile. I loved knowing that what I revealed put that expression on her face.

"Since I know you work for one of the best accounting firms in this state, I'd love to have you check out my small portfolio and make suggestions on where I can improve, readjust, or whatever it is you accountants do to maximize profits for your clients."

"I'd love to, but you seem to be doing well all on your own."

"Coming from you, that means a lot."

She was probably ready for me to get out of her hair, but I wasn't ready. I enjoyed being around her and didn't know how to detach myself from her.

"I'll help you with these dishes, then I'll get out of your hair."

She continued to sit there staring, not saying a word for so long that I squirmed in my seat. She was the only woman I could recall who had the ability to make me nervous.

"We did say that this was a one-time thing. I don't want you to feel obligated to stick around," she finally said.

"Trust me on this, Charla," I picked up our dishes. "I don't feel obligated. I feel lucky."

Her eyes widened at the most honest words I'd spoken since I met her. After depositing the dishes in the dishwasher, I returned to the table. I placed a kiss on the back of Charla's neck like it was the most natural thing I ever did, leaving my lips to linger at her ear.

"I enjoy being around you. A lot."

She didn't reply but stood to join me in clearing the rest of the dishes and loading them in the dishwasher. Once that was done, I located my shoes and socks and prepared to leave. Charla walked me to the door.

After the door was open, I stalled before turning back to face her. I failed to process what I was doing until she was drawn into my tight embrace that forced her to release a cute little giggling gasp.

"I'll see you later. I'll call you," I whispered, clinging to her longer than I intended. My arms were like deadbolts and it took mental strength and physical motivation to let go.

"Okay," she whispered into my neck, embracing me as forcefully as I was her.

I let go and walked away quickly, afraid I would walk right back into her space if I didn't leave fast enough. It hadn't even been a full day, and I was already letting myself get attached.

She hadn't closed her door, and I sensed her eyes on me. Brisk steps weren't getting me to my car fast enough or preventing me from glancing back. Was it possible that I already had feelings for her?

Chapter Twelve

Charla

What the heck just happened? Did my one-night stand just turn into something more? In twelve hours, Ransome and I knew more about each other than some newlyweds. Why the heck had I agreed to see him again? Why did he want to see me again? Why was our connection so familiar and comfortable?

No way was I telling my friends that I allowed what was supposed to be a rebound one-night stand turn into something I couldn't even explain. They would never trust me to date on my own again.

When I finally clicked my phone on, text and missed call notifications made it sound like my phone was belting out a new jingle. There was no use checking the messages. I knew who they were all from.

After a few deep, relaxing breaths, I dialed Callie and Dayton, linking them on a three-way.

"Young lady, you've got some explaining to do," came Callie's motherly tone.

"You don't have to explain shit as far as I'm concerned," Dayton chimed. "If that man just left your house after two p.m., it means you did exactly what you were supposed to do," Dayton continued her encouraging yet misguided speech.

"Ladies. I had a great time with Ransome. We. I. He wants to see me again."

Deafening silence filled the line.

"What!" came from my friends, so loudly I eased back from the phone although it was on speaker. Before they could scold me, I started talking.

"I know the rules. A one-night stand should be just what it is, but he was the one who took my phone and put his number in it right before he made me come for like the fourth time. He also made me promise that it wouldn't be the last time we hooked up. What was I supposed to do at a time like that, say no?"

"Hell, yes, you were supposed to say no. Well... not during, but definitely afterward. After you could think straight, you were supposed to put his ass out and tell him to get lost. The man is a stripper, Charla. He's not dating material. He'll use you until he gets tired, and trust me, his kind will make sure you're good and attached to him when he decides to move on," Callie stated.

It almost sounded like she spoke from experience, but I didn't call her on it.

"Charla, listen," Dayton began, preparing to misguide me even further. "You need to flip the script on his ass. All you have to do is keep emotions out of the equation, and you will be just fine. Use him for sex, and make sure you're the one who turns his ass loose when you've had enough."

It sounded like sound, woman-empowering advice, so I continued to listen.

"There is nothing wrong with you doing whatever the hell you want for a change. Don't let these damn men think they have power over you because they don't. They never have, and they never will. Remember, you're the one with the pussy, and you hold the key to their damn downfall, not the other way around."

Each of my friends had valid points, but it didn't help me feel any less conflicted about what Ransome and I were doing, which I honestly hadn't figured out yet. I liked him despite what he did for a living. Every aspect of him I got to know produced an unexpected surprise. He wasn't his job.

"Did he really make you come four times?" Callie asked. I sensed her wide smile through the phone.

"Five times, actually. Three times last night and twice this morning. The man didn't need instructions. He knew what to do and wasn't all uptight and stingy with relinquishing control either."

"What about the dick girl? Did he have a big one, or is what they say about strippers putting extensions inside those dick strings they parade around in true?"

A splash of warmth raced across my cheeks. Dayton and Callie knew all my business, and I knew all of theirs. Often, they told me too much. So, I didn't feel bad about telling them about Ransome.

"He's *huge*. I'm talking about breaking stereotypes, kind of big. If dancers are putting extensions on their dick, he's not one of them. I had to literally stop and think about whether or not I would be able to handle him."

"Dayam! He was packing like that?" Dayton asked, cackling.

I shook my head, although I knew she couldn't see me. "Yes. It was like that, and as much as I know I shouldn't see this man again, I can't deny the fact that it was…that he was…"

"Better than Carter's old lying ass," Dayton finished. "That bastard only possessed the ability to accidentally make you come anyway."

"Dayton!" Callie shouted through the line.

I didn't correct Dayton because she was right. I was so used to Carter and his selfish sex that I hadn't even acknowledged that our sex life had gotten boring. It was likely only boring to me because Carter would get what he wanted out of it either way.

"Don't 'Dayton' me, Callie. We have been telling this girl for years to find herself someone who could at least make her come right."

I closed my eyes and took a deep breath, glad I had friends who cared about my sex life, if nothing else.

"Ladies, I am going to take a nap."

"He really must have put it on your ass if you're about to take a damn nap at three in the afternoon."

I didn't reply to Dayton's teasing comments.

"Love you, ladies. I'll talk to you later."

"Love you," they sang before hanging up.

Chapter Thirteen

Ransome

Snap! Snap! Snap!

The loud snap of Mark's fingers, one of the talkative dancers, dragged me out of my sluggish haze. He was Asian and African-American, so his exotic features drove the ladies wild. We were in the dressing room preparing for our set, so the rhythm of the music coursing through the place seeped into the area.

"Ran, man, she must have put that magic on you. Your ass has been in a daze since you got here," he quipped with a hungry expression.

And women assumed men didn't gossip. These men discussed who they took home, how good of a fuck they were, what they smelled like, and on and on. There were so many stories about the exploits of some of them that I was sick of hearing them.

It had been a long time since I left the club with a woman, so Mark's comments drew three other sets of eyes in our direction. I sensed that there were now twice as many ears zeroed in on us too.

Although I didn't see any of these guys last night when I left with Charla, I was willing to bet my car that there were multiple sets of nosey eyes on us from inside and outside the building. They were now waiting for me to spill what happened between me and Charla, but I didn't take the bait.

"I'm good, man. Just tired," I said, finally answering him and left it at that.

"Why are you acting all brand new? We saw who you left out of here with. She was fine as hell, but she seemed to be the good-girl type. One of those women who are smart enough not to fall for the likes of one of us. You know, wifey material," he pointed out and didn't mind continuing. "She was one of those types who will get their claws in you so deeply, you'll be quitting this gig, wearing a suit to work every day, and eagerly putting a baby in her."

It sounded like he spoke from experience, but I didn't point it out. He paused and gave me a weird side eye like he knew he'd said too much. A twisted smile formed on his lips at my willful silence.

"Spill it. We damn sure want to know what went down with *her*."

I glanced around at the eager gazes aimed at me. No way in hell I was telling them I had gotten attached to Charla, and on the first night, no less.

"I'm not telling any of you my business," I said.

"Since fucking when? What did that sexy ass woman do to you?" Mark eased back, letting his gaze rake over me. "She was a ten for sure, but damn, she got you acting all secretive like she gave you missile codes and shit. You're seeing her again, aren't you?" Mark questioned.

The curious expressions on the rest of the guys' faces were a clear indication of their eagerness to know the answer, too. This is where I would usually crack and give them a morsel of news, but I couldn't do it this time. My silence prevailed, letting them interpret my evasive demeanor however they wanted.

Mark shook his head, with pity reflected in his gaze. "There goes another one. Not my boy. No. Ran. Damn!" He turned away to reach into his locker, continuing to shake his head and mutter to himself.

Charla did have me in another head-space. All I thought about since leaving her place was calling her to see when I could see her again. Once we got off the subject of her ex, our time together was nothing short of magical.

I shared parts of myself with her and was willing to tell her anything she wanted to know. No one except my two closest friends, Atlas and Trent, knew I was buying a house. Not even these guys nosing in my business right now knew what I did outside the club.

My friends knew my aspirations went far beyond dancing. They knew that I owned a barber shop and had remodeled the two top levels of the same building into four small apartment rentals.

The amount of information I revealed to Charla in such a short amount of time scared the hell out of me. Now, I was about to go out there on stage, and all I could think about was her.

Last night, my interest in her led me to eyeball her mail sitting on her table by the door. Her full name was Charlene McGregor, and her ex was Timothy Carter, who still received mail at her place.

I also noticed the turned-down picture frames of what I assumed were pictures of them together. She hadn't outright gotten rid of them, so the ache of not knowing if she would take him back was a hard punch to my ego.

Forty minutes after my performance, a routine the guys were calling my best yet, I still had Charlene on the brain. The dance steps to my performance had come naturally, and I couldn't recall any of the faces yelling my stage name.

Unbeknownst to her, Charlene had me in a chokehold and wouldn't ease up. The stack of money I had sitting in front of me was one of the highest totals I made so far this year, proving the quality of performance I had given.

What no one knew was that images of Charla filled my head during my performance. She'd been so deep in my head that I was dancing for only her. The sea of women I performed for all had Charla's face. Every curve on their body were Charla's curves. Every move I made was for her. I could hardly wait to see her again and prayed the ex was out of the picture for good.

***

Charla

A week had flown by like a weekend. The best part of it, however, was that Ransome and I spoke to each other every day on the phone and twice when we weren't busy. The idea of getting to know him was foreign at first, but I quickly grew to love our phone chats.

He made me laugh. He could hold a conversation and not make it about sex or him.

Concentrate, I reminded myself. I had gone over my expense reports twice, and each time, I found errors. All that kept popping into my brain was Ransome with his fine and sexy self. And his big—

"Gees, get it together, Charla," I murmured, chastising myself.

I'd gotten to know more about him in the past week than I knew about people I'd known for years. He may be playing me like Callie suggested, but I chose to believe his intentions were genuine.

The way he caressed and kissed me made me feel so wanted. Sincerity had resonated in his tone and in his eyes. It couldn't have all been faked. Could it?

Maybe spending all that time with one man had ruined me. How was I supposed to move on and open myself to anyone else when I was so unprepared and undeveloped for the world of dating?

The best move I knew to make was to seek advice from my friends. One, who suggested I fuck Ransome and leave him, and the other, who suggested I be careful but open-minded.

I believed the best thing I could do for myself was follow my natural instincts and attempt to weed out what I believed was bullshit. I also had to keep in mind that I was vulnerable because my emotions were still raw from my breakup.

After saving my work, I shut my computer down. My attempts at getting anything accomplished had failed, so I headed home.

An hour later, I jumped at the sound of my phone's hard vibration against the end table. I assumed it was Dayton or Callie telling me about the good time they were having at the dance club *Cure*, but instead, it was a text from Ransome.

"Thinking about you. Hope you have a great night."

My smile grew wide. After eleven on a Friday night, he was probably at the club about to make female fantasies come true. I text him back.

"Thinking of you, too."

As soon as my finger hit send, I slammed my eyes shut.

"What are you doing, Charla?" I muttered.

I couldn't keep leading him on like we were in a relationship. I covered my face with the palms of my hands. I had to think about this like a sensible adult. I agreed with my friends that I should tread lightly with Ransome. I was so used to being in a relationship that it was easy to trick myself into believing I was in one now. I wasn't.

Ransome, although he acted the part, wasn't the kind of man who wanted to be in one either. He wasn't going to want what I wanted. I wanted a long-term, serious relationship. I didn't want to be single. I wanted that special person you could share everything with, even those secrets you wouldn't tell your best friends.

My problem was that I didn't feel like going out there and putting in the stressful work of finding a man whose relationship goals aligned with mine.

If Ransome wanted to have sex a few more times, I was all for it, but that was as far as I would let myself go. I had settled for whatever Carter was willing to give me. Now, it was time I got what I wanted from a man.

Chapter Fourteen

Charla

Ransome's call interrupted my Saturday Netflix and chill day. Why was I smiling into the phone like he could see it while the movie I was in the middle of watching sat paused on the screen?

"Are you busy? Can I come over?" he asked, not giving me a chance to make up a lie. My lips twitched. I itched to tell him yes. However, I resisted the temptation and said no. It had only been a week, and I was already aching for him.

"No?" he questioned like he hadn't heard me. "I can't believe you're saying no. I even waited a week to give you time to miss me."

"Well, you better start believing my words because that's what I just said. No." My voice spoke the words, but my heart wasn't in it enough for them to sound convincing.

My leg bounced up and down at the notion of seeing him again. Touching him. Smelling him. Feeling him so deep…

Dammit!

As a matter of fact, my leg jumped so hard that the movement had the lamp rocking on the end table sitting next to the couch.

Thankfully, a knock at my door saved me from the current topic with Ransome.

"Hey, I gotta go. Someone is at my door."

"Okay. I'll call you tomorrow so we can talk about who that was at your door." I didn't miss the tease in his tone.

"Okay, we'll talk tomorrow."

I would rather have stayed on the phone with him than deal with whoever was at my door, but I needed to keep some distance between me and Ransome. I could feel his energy through the phone, so seeing him would only strengthen the strange attachment I was developing.

My heart dropped into my stomach when I spotted who was on the other side of my front door through the peephole. I expected Dayton or Callie, but it was neither. It was Carter.

I stood there, finding interest in the floor patterns. The air around me had stilled, and I didn't know if I was experiencing anger, resentment, or fear. Sound had vacated the premises as well. I wasn't ready to see or talk to him, but my hand found a way to the door, and I fumbled with the deadbolt until it flipped open.

I pulled the door open, and an unusually loud creak sounded like it was announcing Carter's entrance. With my arms folded across my chest, I stepped aside to allow him in. Anger won the contest of raging emotions swirling within me. The feeling ricocheted through me, making me clench my jaw while my gaze raked him up and down a few times.

The jeans and the Burberry button-up I got him for his thirty-sixth birthday three months ago in March were impeccably draped over his tall frame.

When he leaned in and attempted to kiss me, I reared back and eyeballed him like he had lost his damn mind.

"Are you serious right now?" I questioned, my words harsh and sharp. Carter was one of those good-looking men who knew he looked good. His Puerto Rican and African-American roots gave him a *look* that some women, apparently me included, found appealing.

His hair was buzzed low, and his face was always clean of facial hair. His six-foot-two lean frame also added to his appeal. As much as I hated to admit it, I knew I'd been attracted to the way he looked enough to excuse his personality.

He parked himself in the middle of the couch we'd had sex on countless times. Instead of playing the game of having to sit near him based on his positioning, I took the chair that put at least six feet of space between us.

For a reason I couldn't understand, my tiny little cut-off shorts that kept inching up my legs had me feeling like I was in nothing but my underwear. His eyes on my exposed legs and braless chest under my thin tank top didn't feel like it used to. I was—*uncomfortable?*

"Charla, I came here to apologize to you. I was wrong in the way I exited our relationship. I was an asshole, selfish. I didn't think about your feelings, and I am so sorry, baby."

My gaze was stuck on his pinched face, and I couldn't get my vocal cords to align with my mouth to spit out a reply. This was the last thing I expected to hear from Carter, who rarely apologized for anything.

Was he sick, and his new girlfriend didn't want to take care of him?

When he walked out on me a month ago, he was determined to put an end to our relationship, no matter what. It was difficult to believe this was the same person sitting in front of me with stress dominating his facial features.

What had happened to him in the month he'd been gone? I called him. I texted him. I left many messages and received two texts from him telling me we were over and that I needed to leave him alone.

"Why are you here, out of the blue, and apologizing now? Everything you wanted to say has already been said," I told him, my tone edgy and precise.

My question and statement put a deer-caught-in-the-headlights look in his eyes before he plastered a stupid smile on his face. I knew him. He had messed up and now expected me to forgive him and welcome him back. I stared, waiting for the story he'd cooked up. It was liberating to know I could overcome the hold he'd had on me. He cleared his throat when the silence between us grew more intense.

"I was speaking in anger. Had to get my head right. You understand, don't you, Charla?"

My brow lifting was my only reply. The small movement made a crease of concern tighten his face. I bet he was wondering why I wasn't jumping up and down and celebrating his return. Him coming back *was* what I tricked myself into believing I wanted, but sitting here staring at Carter, I accepted he was not what I needed.

"Aren't you going to say anything, Charlene?"

He addressed me as Charlene when he wanted to be taken seriously. I still hadn't answered. Without being aware of when it had occurred, I had purged him from my system.

"I'm sincerely apologizing for the harsh and stupid shit I said to you, for what I did to you, and for leaving you after you'd done so much to make our relationship a success. You supported me through whatever I wanted to do in my career and in life. You cooked for me and my friends, put together parties and events for my employees, found sponsors for my company when some walked away because of my screw-ups, and you believed me over all those jealous people in your ear spreading rumors about me. You probably think I didn't pay attention to all that you did to keep us going, to keep us the couple that others wanted to be like. I appreciate you, Charla, and I'm sorry it's taken me this long to acknowledge it."

My face scrunched into a tight, thinking knot. His words confused me. I swallowed a big gulp of air that had gotten lodged in my throat.

"Thank you for apologizing. I appreciate it, but where is this coming from? You were determined to move on and start a new life, so why would you come back to apologize now after a month? I'm confused."

He wasn't saying so, but something major had gone down with the new lady in his life. I found joy in seeing the misery hidden within the depths of his eyes. His new lady must not have been measuring up. He'd left out a lot in his list of things I did for our relationship. Like all the cooking and cleaning, the ego stroking, and sex even when I didn't want it.

I even put up with his alcoholic father making passes at me that Carter conveniently ignored and cast off as his father's personality. Personality, my ass. The man had felt me up multiple times, and it took me cursing his ass out for him to stop.

"I don't know," he said, finally answering the question I forgot I'd asked. His shoulders remained sitting high. "Sometimes, you convince yourself that you need something, but you already have the thing that you truly need."

What the hell was he trying to say?

Leaning forward, I positioned myself to get a better view of him. I needed to gauge his expression and make sure I understood each syllable of his words.

"What are you saying, Carter?"

"I want you back, Charla. I made a huge mistake when I left you. I'm sorry, baby. I want you back."

He actually had enough nerve to look sincere, but all I kept seeing in my head were the mean looks he gave me when he yelled he didn't want me anymore. I folded my arms across my chest and stuck my chin in the air.

Carter must have been out of his damn mind if he believed it would be this easy to get me back. Before I could stop myself, words were flying out of my mouth.

"I don't want you back. I've had time to think about my life and what I want. I let myself get so involved in pleasing you, lifting you up, and making you happy that I completely forgot about making myself happy in the process."

The shock in his wide eyes and on his frozen face was easy to read. He'd assumed this would be easy, considering how I begged him not to leave me.

He scooted to the edge of the couch, leaning closer in my direction.

"Think on it for a moment, baby, and know that I want to come back home. I made a stupid mistake that I can't take back. I hope you can someday forgive me for being a dick. Please say you'll at least think about it, Charlene."

My anger flared as it was clear that the words I'd spoken so far had gone into one of his ears and out the other one. He spoke like he'd made an honest little mistake. However, the worst mistake he made was ignoring me and giving me time to find something much better than him out there in this world. At this point, I wasn't going to say shit, but what was on my damn mind.

"You left me for another woman who you cheated on me with and got pregnant. You could have given me a fucking disease for screwing her and me without protection. You're having a baby with another woman, and you're here asking me to take you back, to forgive you?"

I jabbed an angry finger in his direction.

"Fuck you, Carter! Fuck you and your sorry-ass apology. Go back to your baby momma."

I stood, my chest rising and falling fast to contain the rage racing through me. My face was so pinched with anger I could hardly see straight as tears blurred my vision.

Carter stood and took quick steps toward the door, eyeing me the entire time. He was not used to hearing me curse at him. Shit, I wasn't used to cursing, but he had it coming.

I didn't bother to see him out either. He knew the way. We were together in this condo for five years. He began turning the door knob but stopped and spun back to face me.

"Please, baby. Think about what I said. I miss you and love you, and made a stupid mistake. I want to come back home, Charlene. We have nearly ten years together, and I don't want to let that go. I want us to get married and plan the family we've always talked about."

I wanted nothing more than to pick up the lamp that caught my eye and heave it at his damn head. *Now*, he wanted to mention marriage after ripping my heart out and tossing it aside.

Folding my arms across my heaving chest, I fell back onto the chair and did my best to keep my raging emotions in check. My right leg jumped wildly, along with a tremble under my right eye I couldn't control. My anger and sorrow were having a boxing match, and I didn't know which of the two would win the fight.

After the lingering silence had sucked the life out of the room, a weird calm settled over me. My tone was low, but my words were serious.

"You don't want me, Carter. You've convinced yourself that you do. You are too weak to overcome your ego, which would let you keep me here unhappy rather than let me move on. But that's okay. We all must face our day of reckoning. Yours has come, and you don't even know it."

My words must have been enough for Carter to get the picture or the calm edge to them freaked him out. I didn't know what had finally silenced him, but I was glad when he turned around and opened that door.

He stepped out and dragged the door closed behind him. He must have paused outside the door because it took a while to hear his footsteps echoing down the driveway.

Carter was right about one thing. I needed time to think. Did I want him back? Ten years was a lot of time to throw away, wasn't it? Was he saying what I wanted to hear so I could take him back? Had he been playing me the entire time we were together? I didn't know what to believe. I didn't know what to think. I didn't know what to do.

Before I called to talk to them about the latest and greatest development in my life, I considered what my friends would tell me. Callie would be the little angel on my shoulder. She would tell me, *"Think about it, weigh your options, and figure out if Carter is who and what you want."*

Dayton would be the little red she-devil on my other shoulder. She would say something like, *"Fuck Carter and the high horse he rode in on. He left. He had his turn and gave it up for a piece of ass that he cheated on you with. Fuck him with a flaming metal dick!"*

Dayton would have no remorse for Carter and would definitely remind me of all the hurt he had caused me. At this point, I had to agree with the little she-devil. I also had to consider how sneaky, vindictive, and determined Carter could be. If he truly wanted me back, this was just the beginning of his quest.

Chapter Fifteen

Ransome

A week later.

Charla hadn't stopped talking to me, but she hadn't claimed me as any more than an extended one-night stand as far as I knew. I wasn't even sure if she saw us as being more than friends. Despite my thoughts on the matter, I called her every day. We enjoyed long and interesting conversations on a large variety of subjects, but I got the impression that she was keeping me at arm's length.

I believed it had everything to do with her ex. The stupid asshole had shown up at her apartment last week, and she hadn't had the same enthusiasm since.

Charla had no idea I had done the one thing I promised I wasn't going to do. I'd sneaked into her apartment complex, intent on walking up to her door and knocking while I had her on the phone. However, her ex beat me to it.

I sat in my car like a dummy, spying on him entering her place with every intention of getting her back. The way he prep-talked himself outside the door revealed to me a man determined to get back what he had so foolishly thrown away.

I studied him extensively, first, by finding his security company's website. Reading his profile gave me an idea of his background as a commissioned officer in the army for eight years. After leaving the military, he established his own security company. Though impressed with his accomplishments professionally and grateful for his service in the military, it was where my appreciation stopped.

I scoured the internet for his social media pages and discovered that he was connected. His personal friends ranked as high as the mayor of the city, the district attorney, and many more who worked for the local police department. He could be seen with some of them in his social media pictures.

If Charla knew I was obsessed enough to spy on her ex, she would dump me for sure. However, I had to know the man who hurt her by cheating and leaving her.

I sat in my car last week cursing, punching the seat, and climbing in and out of the car, stressed about what was happening behind Charla's closed door with her ex. I breathed out a shaky breath of relief, seeing him walk out less than twenty minutes later.

His anger was apparent in his tense body and the way he muttered to himself all the way back to his car. I prayed like I'd never prayed before that Charla would recognize her worth and not go back to him.

Our phone conversations for the past week were the one thin thread of hope I clung to that I still had a chance with her. Whenever I brought up the subject of seeing her again, which was every time we talked, she ignored my inquiry or shut me down. I couldn't blame her. She was fresh out of a ten-year relationship with a man who didn't appreciate her.

If I were being honest with myself, my occupation didn't inspire women to keep seeing me, much less foster a healthy relationship. Charla did, however, answer her phone whenever I called, letting me know she hadn't lost interest.

Now, I called her in the hopes that she would agree to go out.

"Deep inhale and release," I said, coaching myself through a short breathing technique before I dialed her number.

"Hello," she answered on the first ring.

"How are you this fine evening?"

"I'm actually doing well. What about you? Were you able to find the special chair you were trying to get for your shop?" she asked.

During one of our conversations, we discussed some of the updates I wanted to make to my barbershop, and the fact that she listened well enough to ask about it now had me grinning.

"Yes. I found it, and it should be delivered next Wednesday. How would you like to go out to dinner with me to *Pure* on Saturday?" I blurted the request. "I'll even break out my grown-man clothes and wear something to impress you."

She laughed, the sound a sweet one I was in love with. I'd never been to the restaurant—never had a reason to go, but I suggested it in the hope that it would be a place Charla would like.

"In that case, I better break out my little black dress," she replied. The excitement in her voice spiked my positive energy. However, as quickly as she gave me something to smile about, she took it away with her next words.

"Since we agreed during one of our many conversations to be open books with one another, I may as well let you know that Carter stopped by last week. He wants me back."

A long, awkward silence followed those words.

"What do *you* want, Charla? Concentrate only on what *you* want. Not what *he* wants."

Another long pause followed before she answered.

"Honestly, at this point, I don't know what I want. I suggested he go back to his baby momma, and he asked me to think about his proposal to come back."

I prayed she would say that it was me that she wanted, but it was wishful thinking on my part. If I didn't control myself with Charla, I would end up falling hard for her even with her ex still in the picture.

The little voice that fed me the truth yelled, *"You're her rebound, and you've already fallen."*

I ignored the voice. When I was with her, I didn't feel like a rebound. I just felt like *hers*.

"Good for you for not letting him dictate your future," came my delayed response. "Don't let him force you back into something you may not want anymore."

I didn't tell her what I really wanted to say.

"Fuck him! Tell that heartbreaking stupid asshole to kiss your beautiful ass."

I'd had a small sample of Charla, and if that small glimpse into her life was any indication, I didn't want to miss a shot with her because her stupid ass ex was blocking.

"Thank you, Ransome. I didn't expect you to give me that kind of advice. Most guys would have suggested I tell Carter to 'fuck off' or something."

She released a heavy sigh. I waded through all of the things I truly wanted to say about Carter to give Charla the positive feedback she needed to make the best decision for herself, even if it wasn't me.

"As much as I'd love to continue our conversation, I have a busy day at the office tomorrow, so I'm about to prepare for bed. I'll see you in about forty-eight hours."

The idea of linking up with her again had me grinning.

"See you later, Charla. Good night."

I shoved my phone into the back pocket of my jeans and exited my vehicle. My car was the quietest place I could find to talk to Charla. As soon as I pushed the door open, the *thump* of the music and the loud shouts and chatter of the rowdy Thursday night crowd greeted me. I grabbed my duffle from my back seat and headed into the club.

Charla had quickly become my inspiration, not only in dance but in so many other aspects of my life. I wanted her to be proud of me, and since dancing would not inspire pride, I planned to quit as soon as I paid off my house. I was already tripling the payments and could have it paid off in fifteen months if I poured most of my dance money into it.

Charline McGregor, you're going to be mine, even if you don't know it yet. I'd been speaking that aspiration into existence since the night we met.

Chapter Sixteen

Charla

Callie talked my ear off, her words hitting so fast I glanced at her lips to translate everything. While she talked, I got ready for my date with Ransome.

A part of the reason I couldn't keep up with my friend's words was that I was using half of my concentration to contain the bubbling excitement rolling through me at the prospect of seeing Ransome again. However, Callie was worried about me. She came over tonight after I informed her of my plans to have dinner with Ransome.

"Callie, I love you for worrying about me, but we are just going to get something to eat. I'm not dating him. We're not in a relationship. We're not making plans for the future. We're two people who agreed to get together for food. Can a sister eat?"

Callie's unblinking stare stopped me mid-reach for the little black dress I'd picked up on the way home from work. I'd left a few hours early to find the perfect dress with Ransome in mind.

"What?" I asked when it was apparent Callie would stare me down until I withered under her motherly gaze.

"You guys are going to *Pure*, a place *that* upscale doesn't scream, just-linking-up-for-food. Two people linking up for food go to a coffee shop or a diner."

"Callie, if you think I was turning down an invite to a place like *Pure*, you are the one who's crazy. And stop looking at me like I've lost it. In a way, I agree with Dayton. It's time I get the things I want from a man. Right now, I want to have dinner with this hot ass man so we can go to his place or come back to my condo and have a repeat of what we did a few weeks ago."

Callie shook her head before her smile reappeared. She'd concluded she wasn't going to talk her version of sense into me.

"Have fun. Be careful. Call me if you need me. And remember, he's a dancer. They're pros at getting what they want from women and tossing you aside when they are done."

Like at the club, Callie sounded like she'd been hurt by someone like Ransome. She usually shared everything with me, so hopefully, she would eventually share what I suspected may have happened.

"I know, *mom*. I'll be careful. I'll use condoms. And even if I decided to do something dangerous and not use them, the likelihood of me getting pregnant is slim to none. So, don't worry."

My comment about me not getting pregnant put a pitying glint in Callie's eyes that I hated seeing. It was a sore subject that I attempted to make light of when it came up. My inability to conceive had led to me crying on her shoulders countless times throughout the years. She gave me a quick hug and a peck on the cheek before leaving me to finish preparing for my date.

***

My mouth dropped open the moment I opened my front door. Ransome was handsomely dressed in his dark blue designer suit and jet-black tie. His hair was short, but he'd added styling gel that added a sophisticated depth to him that I enjoyed. He resembled a crowned prince of a rich foreign country.

"Wow! You look great. You clean up very well. Come in."

He didn't move. Instead, he stood staring with a huge smile plastered on his face.

"Thank you, but I can't find the right words to describe how gorgeous you are."

My lips spread into a wide grin. The compliment was another one of Ransome's attributes that let me know he appreciated my efforts to look good for him.

"Thank you. Let me grab my bag."

I ran back to my bedroom, checked myself in the mirror one last time, and dashed out to join Ransome. The level of excitement rolling through me had my insides bubbling, and I was unable to be still. A ridiculous smile remained plastered on my face.

Giddiness danced through me and set me on an energetic vibe I prayed would last all night. I hadn't felt this way since I was a teen going out on my first date. In a way, this was a grown-up version of me going out for the first time.

Getting to know someone new was foreign and although it terrified me, I liked Ransome enough that I was willing to set aside my doubts and insecurities and attempt to have a good time.

You can do this, I reminded myself repeatedly before turning and walking out the door with Ransome's hand resting on the small of my back.

On the drive to the restaurant, Ransome had me laughing my lightly made-up face off. The practical jokes he and his dancing buddies often played on each other at the club were our main topic of conversation.

"You put yogurt in the man's G-string and led him to believe that there was a serial masturbater on the loose, shooting their load inside you guy's underwear?"

He chuckled. "Yes. I did it with no shame. Trust me, they have pulled plenty more dirty tricks than that on me."

The drunk antics of the customers they encountered kept me giggling, too.

"One lady had gotten so drunk she somehow got past security and made her way into our dressing room. When she saw all of us in different stages of undress, she started shouting like she was in church with a hand over her chest and the other reaching for the sky while screaming she had stumbled into heaven."

"I'm sorry, but I believe I would have reacted the same way whether I was drunk or not," I told him, giggling.

Once we drove up and stopped at the valet, Ransome walked around to open my door. He took my hand and helped me out of his car. When he planted his hand on the small of my back and escorted me to the entrance, a certain sense of pride filled me.

The restaurant door was opened for us, and a smiling, bright-eyed host greeted and gestured us inside.

The art-inspired decor captured my immediate attention and took my breath away. If a botanical garden and an ancient architectural cathedral had babies, this place would be one of them.

The diners, in various stages of their dining experience, temporarily drew my attention away from the restaurant's impressive interior design. The restaurant was a gallery of expensive showpieces that kept my eyes busy.

Was it me, or were people staring at us like we were celebrities? Their friendly smiles indicated that our presence brought them a sense of joy.

Based on their appearances, the guests were well-to-do upper-middle-class and wealthy types, dressed to impress and flashing black cards. However, based on the smiles that kept coming and the subtle head nods aimed in our direction, Ransome and I fit into the environment nicely. The host greeted us enthusiastically before escorting us to our table.

A reserved sign sat atop our booth that overlooked a lighted, man-made pond filled with beautiful colorful fish. The section of glass flooring beneath our feet gave a clear view of the beautiful marine life aimlessly swimming below us. My breath caught when a five or six-foot shark swam by.

Ransome didn't allow the waiter to assist me into my seat. He did the honor and took his seat before the man placed our menus in front of us. I was too busy staring across the table at Ransome to hear the waiter. He was saying something about wine and a certain dish.

Ransome inclined his head toward the man, letting him know he was free to leave until we were ready to order. I leaned across the table.

"Thank you for bringing me here. I love it."

"Anything for you," he replied, and the confidence in his gaze let me know that he wasn't joking.

This place was within my price range, but Carter and I never really enjoyed places of this caliber. Carter ran his own security firm. He made enough money to spoil me, but he never did because I never required him to go out of his way to make me feel special.

Even when I suggested something as simple as flowers, he handed me his credit card and suggested I have fun. He repeated the sentiment on my birthdays, and instead of demanding more from him, I'd run up his credit card. My spa time, shopping time, and lunch and dinner dates were often with Dayton and Callie.

Through the years, I could count on one hand the number of times Carter and I went out to dinner or to a movie. We made plans several times to take a vacation that didn't involve a weekend in one of his rich friend's hotels or lake houses, but the vacations I was promised never happened. The closest I got was the occasional all-expense four or five-day getaways for Callie, Dayton, and me. The last was to Jamaica. Carter assumed his generosity would buy him favor with my friends, but a dry 'thank you' was all he ever got out of them.

Dayton kept telling me that I had fallen into comfort with Carter. Now, I was starting to believe that maybe she was right. She was sure that while I played Carter's little perfect homebody of a girlfriend, he had a side woman or two that he wined and dined right under my nose.

One look at Ransome and images of the past dissolved. Being around him helped clear my head. Add to that, he'd taken off from work tonight for me. Therefore, I wasn't going to waste his time thinking about what my ex did or didn't do. He leaned across the table, tucking the menu into his chest.

"I don't know anything about pairing wine with food, so will you help me pick?" he asked, not the least bit afraid to admit what he didn't know.

"Of course. What are you having?"

"It's been a while since I've had fish. I think I'll have the Chilean sea bass, veggies, and roasted truffle potatoes. What about you?"

"This lobster and scallop pasta is calling my name." I reached for the wine menu and glanced through it. "The simple rule to remember when pairing wine is red meat, red wine, and white meat, white wine unless you have an experienced palate and know all the nuances of the flavor mixtures. That being said, I would suggest a glass of this Pinot Noir for us. It's light, not too sweet, and will bring out the flavor in your food."

The waiter must have been standing in a corner waiting for us. As soon as we were sure about what we wanted, he walked up to the table, his smile reaching us steps ahead of him. Once we'd ordered our food, I asked, "What made you pick this place?"

He shrugged. "Because I thought you'd like it."

I considered his words, appreciating his thoughtfulness.

"What about me made you think I'd like this place."

A shriek of embarrassment crossed his face and disappeared quickly.

"Because you're classy, kind of prissy even, but not in the stick-up-the-butt way that's unapproachable. You're also incredibly sexy, you have flavor and style, and although you've been through hell with your ex, you continue to hold your head up with a level of confidence that not many women have. I've never been to this place, but everything I researched about the scenery, the vibe, and the food kind of reminded me of you."

"You think all of that about me?" I asked. His words had me breathless. No man had ever described me in such detail in such a sweet way, aside from the prissy part. How could he think this much of me in the short time we'd known each other?

"Yes," he answered. "Before I suggested it, I assumed you'd tell me you've been here before."

I shook my head, "No. This is my first time, and I'm glad you chose it for us."

Dinner with Ransome turned out magnificently. The wine, the great food, and his insightful conversation made the night a memorable one. We even shared a delicious chocolate souffle for dessert. Each moment I spent with this man made me want to dive deeper into his world, but I fought the impulsive urge. I couldn't allow myself to get attached to Ransome, but I'd be damned if he wasn't making it hard. I *liked* him more than I was willing to admit to myself.

Why was I kidding myself? I fell in lust with the man as soon as he climbed into my bed. The idea that he was genuinely interested in me made the use-him-and-leave-him attitude I was supposed to have much harder to pull off.

Ransome didn't give off the vibe of someone who was about to use me and throw me away, but what did I know? I didn't have any dating experience to fall back on to tell me if I was being stupid or just plain dumb where this man was concerned. I'd dated a few guys before Carter, but at that time, I was a teen who guarded my virginity like it was the holy grail.

Lost in my head, I remained silent for most of the drive back to my place.

"Can I ask you a question that I would like an honest answer to?" I asked Ransome out of the blue.

He took his eyes off the road to glance in my direction.

"You can ask me anything, and I will always be honest?"

Let's see how honest he would be after I asked my question.

"I don't have an extensive resume of men I've dated, so I can't really take an educated guess as to what we, me and you, are doing. It doesn't feel like we're just hooking up. What do you want from me? Is it just sex until you grow tired of me?"

"No, Charla. You're not even close. The first night we met, you had the power to claim my attention in a crowded, dark club while I danced. I had to meet you after I left that stage. When I was talking to you, I promise, you were the only woman I saw in that club. I wanted to be in your space. I wanted to know more about you. I am genuinely interested in you."

He paused, flashed me another quick glance, and a sincere smile.

"Considering where we met and what I do for a living, I didn't think someone like you would take me seriously. I went along with the one-night stand you proposed hoping that you'd actually see past my occupation and see me. I hoped, still hope actually, that you see more in me than just a stripper. I have goals, dreams, and so much more I want to accomplish, and it would be nice to have someone to share those accomplishments with."

That was a damn good answer. I bit into my bottom lip before I responded. "So, just to be clear, you're looking for more than a fling?"

"Yes. Like I said the night we met, I honestly have a different kind of agony. Despite what I do, I lead a lonely life. I want to go home to someone at night who cares about how my day went. I want someone I can tell my secrets, fears, and successes to. I want to be wanted for something other than my body or the amount of money some women think I might spend on them. I want more than what I've been getting."

I wrinkled my brow. "And you think I can give you that?"

"Yes," he answered with no hesitation.

"Even after what I told you about my ex trying to get me back?"

He placed his warm hand on my leg but kept his eyes on the road.

"You gave me more than any woman in less than twenty-four hours. Conversation. Interest. Respect. Your secrets. And despite what we agreed to at the club, you didn't look at me like I was a prop you were about to use for sex and be done with. Therefore, I'll take whatever time you're willing to spend for as long as it lasts."

I didn't know how to respond to him. I appreciated and understood what Ransome was telling me. I felt the same, but there was so much more to consider, like the fact that I didn't believe I was ready or mentally prepared for another relationship. Ransome was everything a significant other should be, but I had to consider that I thought the same about Carter when we first met.

Ransome and I had hardly scratched the surface of each other. My eyes fell closed on a deep inhale. Every time I was sure I had things organized in my head, I found that I wasn't even close to putting things into perspective.

I connected with Ransome in a way I couldn't describe—in a way I was afraid to admit out loud. Ransome remained silent while my rambling thoughts resumed their duty of consuming me.

Chapter Seventeen

Charla

Time passed in a blur, and the next thing I knew, the familiar surroundings of my neighborhood filled my view. Ransome punched in the code to my gate without asking for the numbers. The keypad beeped for each number he tapped before he drove us toward my condo. He parked, and like the first time, he kept me in place with a calm hand on my arm.

"Let me," he insisted, stopping me from opening my own door. I loved his gentlemanly ways. At first, I assumed it was an act, but I was learning that chivalry was a genuine part of Ransome's attitude.

When he took my hand to help me out of his car, a jolt of an unseen force shot up my arm and sent a chill racing up my spine. He must have felt it, too, because his eyes locked with mine, and we stood in place, staring at each other in a moment that stretched on for an eternity.

I cleared my throat before stepping away from him to head toward my front door. We entered in silence. Ransome closed and locked my door, a sign that he had no intention of leaving right away.

When I sat my purse and keys on my door-side table, the warmth of his body behind mine made me sigh. He reached around me and placed his car keys next to my purse. In one swift motion, his soft lips swept the expanse of my neck, stealing my breath while his strong hands wrapped around my waist.

"You're beautiful. And so sexy."

His words slid against my neck, and the next thing I knew, he spun me around so fast that my gasp whipped through the air. Reaching low, he gripped the hem of my dress and proceeded to drag it up my legs with deliberate intent. Heat rose within my belly, and the flames from his perusing eyes threatened to consume me.

My mind flew out the window and left my body to fend for itself. My heart hammered out its raging rhythm against my breastbone. A chill rolled through me, making my skin prickle, all while my body caught fire from the heat Ransome gave off.

Nipples tight, pulse jumping, and juices flowing, he controlled me with every stroke and hot caress. His soft lips traced their way down my neck and chest while my dress was being steadily lifted, his fingertips flirting with my skin the whole time. The cool breeze flowing through my living room took the place of his kisses against my skin while I lifted my arms to make it easier for him to peel my dress off.

A little whimper bubbled up in my throat when he tugged me into his strong body and covered my lips in a firm kiss. I groaned against his mouth and assisted him when he backed away enough to strip off his jacket.

Before the jacket hit the floor, I was working on the buttons of his shirt. He helped me by ripping the shirt open with one quick yank that sent buttons flying everywhere. The sight caused a storm of wetness to pool in my already damp panties. While he dropped what was left of his shirt, I worked on getting him out of those pants, my uncoordinated fingers failing to get the job done fast enough.

His eyes never broke their connection with mine when I lowered, kept my neck angled up to watch him and worked his pants down his legs. The sight of his hot, wet tongue sliding across his bottom lip made me groan. Fuck the pants. I left them around his ankles like he'd done my jeans the night we met. I went for his briefs, taking them down past his knees in an anxious frenzy.

With his legs trapped in his pants and briefs, I had him temporarily locked in place. I filled my hands, massaging the prize that had given me so much pleasure a few weeks ago. My lips pressed against the precum-drenched tip, and I couldn't help tempting my eager tongue.

The swollen pink head, hot and pulsing against my tongue, leaked a trail of his warm, sweet nectar. Ransome took in a deep chest-heaving breath at the sight of my lips wrapping around his tip before his eyes slammed shut. The sight of his muscles tensing and releasing encouraged the ravenous mouth action I lavished on his dick.

Was a man supposed to taste this damn good? His flavor reminded me of refreshing peach tea. My lips spread wide around his thickness, and I slurped and licked up his shaft until the head struck the back of my throat. My mouth became as wet as my pussy had gotten.

His dick, so thick and long, forced me to use my hands to massage the bottom half of his shaft while my mouth feasted on the top half. As for the portion I worked with my mouth, I twirled my wet tongue one moment and relaxed it the next to spread my attention around him.

Ransome appreciated my efforts enough to tell me how good I was doing.

"Yes, baby. Suck that dick. Fuck. It looks so good disappearing into your sweet mouth."

The thrill and self-gratification from doing my job had saliva drizzling down my chin. It was possible I enjoyed this as much as Ransome. I moaned right along with him as I sucked and slurped on his dick like I was determined to win a contest.

I continued to receive rave reviews from Ransome, the man attached to the only other dick I ever had in my mouth. I usually didn't enjoy giving oral. But with Ransome, the act was a pleasing build-up to what was to come. Add to that, the man's dick was flavorfully delicious, a flavor I would gladly use as my own personal mouthwash.

"Charla. Ba-be-ee," he stretched the word baby out like he was hurt and needed to be rescued. Trembling legs, heaving chest, and his abs pulled tight enough to snap, added to my already flowing confidence.

He gripped the side and back of my head, urging me to go faster. I gave him what he wanted while glancing up to meet his heavy eyes whenever I wasn't choking on his dick. Desperately, I needed to see him come in my mouth as badly as I knew he wanted to.

"Shit, I'm about to come," Ransome whispered in a harsh breath, eyes wide, and body so tight every muscle was working at the same time. He was forced to reach and grip the edge of the table to remain on his feet.

"Shit. Charla. Oh, shit, baby," he said between hisses and other slurred words. When his warm juice flowed into my mouth, so sweet and tasty, I didn't mind swallowing. I moaned with every shot he sent into my mouth.

"Oh. Shit," he said, his mouth open, eyes wide, and chest pumping in wild exhilaration. Seeing me swallow his come sent a few more hot shots into the back of my throat. Ransome's body trembled so badly it appeared he was having a seizure.

I didn't release his dick from my mouth's hungry grip until I was sure I'd sucked him dry. I went as far as licking every inch of his semi-erect dick, not wanting to leave any of his flavor behind.

When I finally turned his dick loose, he glanced down, lips parted, eyes unblinking and face flushed. Satisfaction sparked in his glazed eyes as he continued to grip the table. His eyes hung so heavy I believed one blink would induce sleep. He managed to release the table and stood upright before he took my hand and stumbled to my couch with me in tow.

I plopped down next to him, intending to let him recover, but he drew me into his chest and placed a kiss on my forehead. His breathing continued to flow in quick, breathless spurts.

"That was amazing. You are amazing." He sighed the words and drew me in tighter. "Honest truth, that was the best blow job I've ever had in my life."

He kissed me again, keeping me pinned to his chest when our lips separated.

"Thank you," I said, skeptical of the compliment. Surely, with all the women he had access to, I couldn't have been the best oral sex he'd had. Then, an idea hit me. I raised my head from his chest and stared at the side of his jaw.

"Ransome," I called his name with an edge of curiosity riding my tone.

"Yes," he answered, stretching the word out playfully.

"How old are you?"

He laughed. "Does it matter?"

I shrugged, "I guess not, but I'm curious."

I sensed that he was younger than me, but I couldn't put my finger on how many years. He slid off the couch and assumed a kneeling position in front of me before dragging me into position in front of him. He was man-handling me the way I secretly liked but had never admitted out loud.

Warm lips grazed my exposed stomach before he worked his way down to my thigh. He gripped either side of my panties and tugged, and I easily lifted to make his job easier. I hadn't given him a blow job so he could reciprocate and eat my pussy, but I damn sure wasn't going to stop him.

"I'll tell you how old I am after I eat your pussy. Then you can tell me if it matters."

At this point, I couldn't care less about age. He slid my panties down my legs with an expression that said he was about to make me forget that I even asked him a question.

Completely naked, I was spread before him like a feast he'd prepared. As soon as his lips brushed my inner thigh, I sucked in a breath and melted into the couch cushions.

He shoved my left leg back before draping it across his shoulder. My right foot was placed on the couch and pushed away from my body, spreading me open for what he was preparing. He lowered his head but managed to keep his eyes locked on mine. The sight of his mouth inching closer to my pussy with my legs spread wide had me dripping wet.

His warm breath brushed my core before his sexy lips connected with my lower ones. He kissed my pussy first, sending a hot shot of lust up my center. Next, his tongue introduced itself, and the sight of it brushing up my brown lips before dipping deeper was almost as erotic as it felt. A moan formed in my throat but didn't make it past my lips.

His tongue action mesmerized me, and the visual of his lazy flicks added more depth to the sensation that had my eyes rolling to the back of my head. My loud moans echoed throughout the room, the sensations so intense my nails dug into the couch's velvety upholstery.

"Yes. Yes!" I chanted before a deep, satisfying gasp stopped my shouts. The man could eat pussy as good as he fucked. Why was he so good at everything? I believe his intention was to make it difficult for me to walk away when the time came.

My tits bobbed up and down in an attempt to keep up with my harsh breaths that felt like they were being yanked from my lungs by Ransome's magnificent performance. My core, as well as my entire lower region, flooded with so much pleasure that I flowed like liquid heat under his control.

Ransome ate me with gusto and purpose, his mouth, tongue, and face buried in my wet folds. His strong arm was clamped around the leg he draped across his shoulder to keep me where he wanted me while he enjoyed his feast.

He lifted his head, flashing a view of his eyes and his tongue dancing around my clit. His palm slid down the leg splayed against the couch and didn't stop until his middle and ring finger were positioned below his mouth at my hot opening.

He ate away my ability to form words and left me to communicate with frantic pelvic maneuvers, urging him to proceed with whatever he intended to do next. When he shoved his long fingers inside me and delivered firm licks all around my clit, my ass cheeks tightened, and my lower body lifted from the couch, chasing the hot currents flowing through my possessed body.

The flick of his tongue, coupled with the movement of his fingers in and out, did me in. He curved one stroke and straightened the next, then blessedly repeated. I couldn't take it anymore. A dam of passion broke loose and caused my pelvis to dance against Ransome's face, my hips thrusting up to make sure my clit kissed his tongue and his fingers delved as deep as they could go.

His velvety tongue and his fingers stroking my G-spot overloaded my senses. I lost it all, mind, body, and all sense of time.

With my fingers buried in his hair, I gripped his head, holding on to make sure he didn't take away the best thrill of my life. I was unaware of how possessed I'd been until I fell back onto the couch with a sigh, shivering through the intensity of my satisfaction.

I blew at the loose strains of my hair, hanging limp over my face. My breaths hissed as a gradual smile formed on my face.

"Oh my God," I whispered through harsh breaths. My heartbeat thrummed through me, the sound loud in my ears.

Ransome continued to sop up my juices with me splayed deliciously open for him while my blown mind was being lured back into my head. Each time his slow tongue lapped up the last remaining traces of my orgasm, I jumped from the contact and the aftershocks that continued to course through me.

What was this man doing to me? That orgasm almost took my life. I was sure my heart stopped a few times.

One last lingering kiss was placed on my still pulsing core before Ransome raised himself onto the couch to sit beside me. We sat staring at the ceiling for a long moment before either of us said a word.

Relaxed—boneless is a more accurate description as I didn't have the strength even to close my legs. My eyes drooped, heavy with satisfaction, but I fought the haze threatening to take me under. I wanted to do more to Ransome, and I wanted him to do more to me in return.

I finally gathered enough strength to close my legs before I let them drop and hit the floor with a solid thump. I lulled to the right until my head fell against Ransome's shoulder. He tucked me against him until my head rested against his chest. His heart didn't thump loudly but fluttered rapidly under my cheek.

Us together like this after having mind-blowing sex was, hands down, one of the best non-sexual sensations I'd ever experienced. Now, I understood the sentiment, why so many couples cuddled after sex. It was a whole different vibe, much like a soak in a tub after a hard, pressing day.

Chapter Eighteen

Charla

Warm lips caressed my forehead, luring me back to reality and away from the stupor I was a few breaths from sliding into.

"You're not falling asleep on me, are you?"

"Heck no," I answered quickly.

His question gave me the spark of anticipation I needed to continue this escapade. I stood and glanced back at Ransome, gesturing my head toward my bedroom for him to follow me. My gaze dropped away from his and landed on his stiff dick. He was ready for me. The teasing glint in his eyes and his telling smirk had me grinning from ear to ear.

Yummy!

The man was sexy and delicious enough for me to commit several gluttonous sins.

With only his body language, he set my juices flowing down to my pussy so fast, and I had no idea where all that sexual energy came from so suddenly.

As soon as we marched through the bedroom doorway, he spun me to him, making me collide with his solid frame with a loud smack. His lips were on mine within seconds, his mouth and tongue claiming mine as savagely as he had claimed my lady parts. He lifted, and my legs wrapped around his tight waist, automatically caging him to my body.

He continued to devour my lips and mouth as we crept through the dark room. I don't know how he remembered my bedroom's setup so well, but he clicked on my lamp without missing a beat.

His tongue slid possessively along mine as I danced anxiously against his stiff member. I'd all but forgotten about protection until he slid my bedside dresser open. He reached in blindly and extracted the box of condoms we'd started on a few weeks ago.

I devoured his neck as he ripped the condom wrapper open and proceeded to reach under my ass to roll it on. Next thing I knew, he placed a hand under my ass, lifted, and brought me down on his thick dick.

"Oh God," flew out of my mouth. I was not ready, but I was hungry for him to fill me up just the same. My hand slapped against his back as I adjusted my hold around his neck and maneuvered my lower body to assist him in readying me for deeper penetration. We remained standing, indulging in the heat of our passion for a few minutes before he climbed into bed, still deep inside me.

He laid me on my back and began a thrusting rhythm that had me clawing at his skin and gripping the fresh comforter I'd put on my bed that morning.

"Jesus, I've been missing out. Your dick is like magic. It feels so good."

Maybe I shouldn't have been saying this out loud, but I couldn't help it. He knew how to get me into that zone where I was prone to say out loud whatever I was thinking.

"You feel good, too, baby. The best I've ever been with," he whispered his words into my ear. Then proceeded to kiss me as he screwed me into my mattress. It only took minutes, and the next thing I knew, Ransome made me come so hard and long and good that I think I blacked out for a second.

By the time I lifted my eyelids, he'd gotten up and was back in the room, handing me a glass of water. I couldn't remember anything past the orgasmic lean he'd put me in.

I accepted the water with a smile, not letting on that he'd fucked me so good, I lost a little time.

"Thank you."

"My pleasure," he replied with a ready smile before climbing back into bed. I guzzled the water, taking it down around my heavy breaths, and didn't stop until the glass was empty. Ransome took the glass when I sat there with it empty in my hand. It was like my brain couldn't process what I should do next.

He picked up a bowl of grapes and strawberries from my nightstand that he must have brought in with the water.

"We didn't have enough dessert tonight. And I have it on good authority from the insightful conversations that we've had that you have a sweet tooth," he said as he fed me a grape.

We had dessert, all right. The best kind.

"Thank you." I bit into a strawberry and licked his finger after biting off half the fruit. Once I'd devoured every strawberry and grape in the bowl aside from the few Ransome ate, he drew me into his chest and pulled the covers over us.

His attentiveness filled me with a level of contentment I'd never experienced. I wasn't greedy, but if I could get this level of attention and affection twice or even once a month, I would be a very happy woman.

We talked briefly about how busy work was now that I was diving into a new account. Ransome wanted more details. His interest made me want to share with him, so I let it all spill out, talking low into his strong chest.

"Have you given any thought to what you might do about Carter?" Ransome asked.

I grew quiet. My mind froze before I acknowledged that I hadn't considered Carter's proposal of us getting back together. Ransome was the man in my bed, so I could imagine he wanted to know where he stood in this equation.

"Carter called me at work a few days after he showed up here, pressuring me again to take him back. He was charming at first, making promises and claims of how much he'd changed in the last month. When his charming act didn't help him get the answer he wanted to hear, he became more demanding and forceful. It got to the point that I eventually hung up on him. He called enough times that I had my receptionist block his incoming calls into our office."

"It's harassment. Do you need help getting him off your back?"

"No. I appreciate you asking, but Carter is going through growing pains because he's used to getting his way with me and almost everyone else in his life. He has to learn that he can't always get what he wants. I have to learn to say no to him, and lately, it's been easy."

"Remember to do what makes you happy. Put yourself first in every decision you make."

I nodded, noticing he hadn't requested that I leave Carter but instead suggested I put myself first. Why couldn't I have met Ransome under a different set of circumstances?

I didn't tell him, but I'd also had to turn off the sound on my cell, and by the time I stepped out of the office that day, Carter had left thirty texts and ten missed calls. Carter was harassing me, but I wondered if I secretly liked the idea of him begging and bugging out because he wasn't getting his way.

If he didn't get what he wanted, when he wanted it, he'd stop at nothing until he did. It's one of the reasons his security firm was so successful. Carter had also done some vicious things to make his firm a success, including sabotaging his competitors' chances of winning contracts, stealing employees, and other tactics I hadn't known about until his friends accidentally let them slip in front of me.

The air of unpredictability about Carter gave me pause to tread lightly against his attempts to win me back. Ransome and I would soon end our affair and never see each other again, so there was no need to drag him any further into me and Carter's drama. I already feared I'd said too much.

Once the conversation dwindled, Ransome kissed my forehead.

"Get a little nap so your body will be prepared for round two."

I lifted my heavy head, kissed him on the cheek, and prepared for the nap he suggested. I was willing to give him a round two, three, or eight if he wanted it.

I didn't know what to do about Carter. I didn't know what I would do about Ransome. Up until he walked into my life, I was a hot mess, feeling sorry for myself over a man who wanted to keep me because time was the only legitimate reason he had for preserving our relationship.

Ransome made me happy. He listened when I spoke. He cared about what I needed. If I was being completely honest with myself, I needed Ransome in my life.

Chapter Nineteen

Charla

My eyes snapped open and landed on Ransome's handsome face. His prize-winning smile lit up my bedroom, his face resting inches away from mine.

"You're so beautiful. One more time," he said. The pleading glint in his gaze made my forehead crease. After having woken me twice last night for multiple rounds of the best sex of my life, he still wanted more.

I was willing to give him what he wanted but didn't want him to notice my eagerness, so I faked a yawn before giving in. All it took was one lazy roll of my ass against what was pressed snuggly against it.

"This time, I'll go slowly. I'll make love to you," he added in a placating tone. I believed on some level he feared that I was getting tired of him.

The dim light of dawn alerted me that it was sometime between five and six in the morning. One of our escapades had gotten so wild we knocked the alarm clock and the expense report I was working on off my nightstand.

"You sexed me into another world, fucked me into oblivion, took me in ways I've never been taken before, and now you want to make love to me?"

He shook his head, his deep smile highlighting the curious glint shining in his eyes.

"We're doing what we want without regard to set standards that most people break anyway." It was so hard to say no to that damn smile of his.

"Can I make love to you, Charlene?"

Damn. He'd called me by my full name, and the seriousness in his voice was unlike his usual playful and amusing tone. I reached back and tossed the covers off my naked body before wiggling my ass suggestively.

"I'm all yours."

A smile spread across his face, and his eyes lit with a vibrancy I never saw in them before. He ran a slow hand down the length of me, from the back of my shoulder, down my bare back, over my right ass cheek, and finally down the back of my leg.

He studied me, eyeing every area he stroked before leaning down to place a soft kiss on my ass cheek. A trail of goosebumps was left every place his lips caressed.

He stopped me from sitting up by placing a firm hand on my back before letting it slide down until he was cupping my cheek in his palm. The intensity with which he stared into my eyes caught me off guard. His brows pinched and his gaze searched, unearthing emotions I was determined to keep buried in the locked closet inside my head.

This intense caress of his and his lingering gaze made this encounter different—more impactful. I glanced away to avoid him seeing the intoxicating emotions he pulled from an unexplored place inside me.

When he leaned in and kissed me again, my lips melted against his before he eased his tongue into my mouth. I moaned, not because I was aroused, but because of the mix of emotions that had my stomach fluttering like a flock of energetic birds had taken flight.

Ransome didn't care that he was revealing how much he cared with his touch or his emotion-filled gaze. Was I reading him right? Was it love reflected in his gaze?

No way!

I was reading too much into this. I was experiencing too much at once. Maybe I was concentrating too hard. I needed to close my eyes and let the moment flow naturally without hammering mental nails into it.

Ransome laid me flat on my back and proceeded to awaken every nerve with delicate kisses, steady flicks of his hot tongue, and lazy strokes of his fingers. Once I was as calm and relaxed as I'd ever been in my life, he laid his body against mine.

His legs rested against the outside of mine, keeping them closed. He wasn't ready for that part yet. He kissed me instead.

Starting with my neck, he triggered my erogenous zone, his tongue sliding over my pounding pulse point. Electricity raced straight down to my core, awakening my arousal in that area, too.

Next, he concentrated on my nipples, biting, teasing, and licking them to the point of adding more fuel to my burning arousal below. He pleasured my stomach and legs and even sucked on my toes until I flowed with a magnetic chemistry that only he could induce.

This was way more intimate than any of our previous encounters. It felt personal. Was this intimacy? If so, I had to accept that I'd never experienced it before Ransome.

The ex's idea of making love was screwing me slower than usual. His idea of being intimate was giving me one of his quick back rubs. How could I be this damn old and not have known this side of romance?

When Ransome made it back up to my mouth, I was so wet and ready for him the mere act of him filling me was probably going to make me come. He didn't go for it right away after he slipped the condom on.

He calmed me with a sensual kiss. Then, with his body splayed against me, he used his legs to ease mine apart. His hard erection landed right at my hot, wet core. I eased my pelvis upwards, desperate for him to fill me up like only he could.

He caressed my chin and turned my face until our eyes locked. His other hand brushed along my thigh and went for the area I wanted him to stroke next. With his eyes deadlocked on mine, he eased back and sank into me with such a slow, powerful thrust that I cried out his name in a strangled whisper.

"Ran...some."

I wanted so badly to close my eyes to the blissful sensation of him sliding in, slow and deep, but I couldn't. Our eyes were locked in a hold stronger than any physical touch. I wanted to see what he was experiencing as much as his intrigued expression suggested he wanted to know what I felt.

No one had ever poured this level of care into me, shared this much emotion, or allowed me to see this level of vulnerability. Carter had taken my virginity, but Ransome was taking much more. Ransome was taking my heart.

He continued to ply me with deep, lingering thrusts. His hands left my chin and thigh, and he sought out my hand and interlocked our fingers. If we weren't kissing each other, we were staring into each other's eyes, sharing a connection that I was sure I wasn't imagining any more.

The longer we remained in this world together, the more emotions surfaced, and the more I accepted what I was experiencing.

Love.

The knowledge of it frightened me so badly I closed my eyes and turned my head away.

"Look at me, Charlene."

Those were the first words either of us had spoken in a while. I shook my head, deathly afraid to let him see what I felt.

Did he already know? Did he know that I was falling for him? I shut my eyes tighter when my heart continued to betray me. Its erratic thumping, along with my breathlessness, was a dead giveaway.

I'd lost control the moment I glanced into Ransome's eyes. When I finally found the courage to meet his waiting gaze, what I found was no longer hidden within their depths. I gasped.

This fling I was having wasn't about me losing control. This was me losing my heart to a man I was supposed to be having fun with.

Ransome caught me in a heart-stealing kiss at my attempt to turn away again. The energy stirring between us sent me on an emotional frenzy and delved so deeply into me, tears stung my eyes.

He captured my moans between tender kisses and continued to work my body, sending layer after layer of pleasure into my core as he made passionate love to my mind above.

I was so overcome with pleasure and raw emotions I stopped fighting it. I exploded into a brilliant array of powerful sensations that rocked me and ripped through me.

Ransome met me in this sensational place as our bodies trembled until the currents eased and released us. Shivers still rolled through me at the delicate press of his warm lips on my neck. The sizzling passion between us hadn't faded.

Ransome rolled me along with him, tucking me in so that my head rested on his chest. I slung my relaxed arm across his stomach and my leg over his. Why did this feel so good, so right, so relaxing?

"Was that okay," he asked. His words were a whisper against my cheek.

"That was perfect," I stated truthfully. My words brought a smile to his lips, and he turned into me, wrapping me in a strong embrace. His mouth was right at my ear.

"I love you."

Those three words. The way he'd said them. The emotion he expressed them with. Those words sent an electrifying buzz into me with a strength that would have knocked me down if I were standing. I was helpless to do anything but absorb the shock. This indescribable, relentless feeling was ripping me apart. I'd never experienced it before. I'd never experienced these strong currents. I lay there stunned beyond words.

I don't know what the hell happened next. I slung my arms around Ransome's neck and buried my face between his neck and chin, reveling in the feel of him wrapped around me so tightly. I burrowed deeper into that feeling he gave me.

"I love you too," tumbled across my tongue. I sucked in a harsh breath and ceased all movement like it had the ability to blink away my slip-up.

What the fuck was going on? Did I just tell Ransome that…that *I loved him*?

When he began peppering my face with kisses and laughed with the giddiness of a playful child, I knew I'd spoken my declaration out loud. Had I just lied to Ransome about love?

I told him that I loved him without admitting the terrifying revelation to myself. I hadn't yet accepted it fully, so was it the truth, or was I just caught up in the moment?

I jumped out of his embrace and backed away. My back collided with the headboard, and I stared at Ransome's stunned face with wide eyes. My hand cupped my forehead as my elbows landed on my knees. My breaths heaved and got worse, making my chest bob hard and fast. That's when I noticed I was shaking.

What had I done? What had I confessed? I was never supposed to tell Ransome how I was feeling because I didn't trust my emotional state right now. It was supposed to stay inside my head where it belonged.

"Ransome. What are we doing? We...just...me." I was so damn mentally disoriented I had trouble spitting out my words. "We are supposed to be having fun. I know what I just said to you, but I don't think I knew what I was saying. I think I was caught up in the moment. I don't want to lead you on about anything.

"Shit!" I cursed to myself, my head hanging low to my chest from the heavy impact of my racing thoughts. "I still have my ex to deal with. We can't be more than...than..."

No matter how hard I fought it, emotions crept from every word, backing up those three sacred words I'd spoken to Ransome moments ago.

Ransome gripped my shaking hand, soothing me. His reassuring smile calmed me even more. The light stroke of his thumb rubbing across the back of my hand added to the campaign to brush away the panic.

"I know this is scary. I know you have a lot to deal with. I also know that I love you, Charlene. You don't have to love me back right now if you need time to figure things out. I'll wait for as long as you need me to, and if you decide I'm not what you want, then I'll deal with it."

A tear slid down my cheek.

"I'm so sorry, Ransome. This…"

"I know," he said when I couldn't finish my sentence. "This is sudden. Too much too fast."

He drew me in close enough that I was able to rest my head on his chest before I wrapped my arms around his torso. We remained in a tight embrace for a long moment.

"I'm going to get out of your hair and give you some room to breathe," he stated.

When Ransome released me from his embrace and eased from my bed, I think my heart went with him. My heartbeat thumped, but my chest felt vacant and empty now. I didn't want him to go, but I couldn't expect him to stay when I didn't know what the hell I wanted.

His big droopy eyes. His dragging movements. His care to avoid glancing my way. I'd hurt his feelings.

The last thing I wanted to do was hurt him. He was always good to me, and I believed good for me. He stood in my bedroom doorway and glanced back at me.

"I'll call you later."

All I could do in reply was nod and avoid his eye contact. Once my front door closed, I slid back under the covers and pulled them over my head. What the hell had I done?

Chapter Twenty

Charla

The next day brought a different kind of drama. Carter. He was relentless in his pursuit and hadn't let up one bit in his quest to win me back. The script had been flipped. Carter was getting a taste of what I lived through for a month. The notion brought me a sick sense of pleasure I wasn't ashamed to admit liking.

Over the course of the following week, I allowed at least twenty of his calls to go unanswered. I replied to two of about a hundred of his text messages. *"I don't want to talk right now,"* is the message I'd left him each time.

The truth of the matter was Ransome was who consumed my thoughts. He texted me twice a day to check on me, and I immediately texted back. Regarding our relationship status, he placed the ball in my court and hadn't mention it.

Although it was difficult to process, I believed I'd needed the shock of Carter's betrayal and abrupt departure to reset my relationship thought process. I needed the hurt to start learning and figuring out what I needed from a man, mentally and physically.

Looking back at my life, I believe I was using my friends to fulfill my mental and social needs, which was okay, but I also needed a mental connection with the man in my life. Conversating and getting to know Ransome allowed me to see that I'd never had that part of me properly fulfilled.

My father walking out on my mother when I was seven and never returning wasn't as devastating to me as my mother had assumed. He had never fathered me, had never supported or given my mother what she needed. He cheated, belittled her, and looked at us like we were his greatest burdens. When he left, my mother cried and wallowed in depression for a few months, but I never saw her more alive than when it was just me and her.

She never found the nerve to get back out there and find someone she could spend the rest of her life with. Had my mother been sick, even back then? I also couldn't help thinking that it was me who kept her from pursuing a long-term relationship. Instead of finding her a special someone, she poured all of her energy into me and her career.

Despite her decisions, she repeatedly made me promise not to give up on finding someone to love. Someone worthy of me. Someone who took care of me spiritually, mentally, and physically. She forced me to say that I would keep trying even if the first two or three relationships failed. It was only now that I understood why she forced me to make those promises.

She even warned me to stay clear of the ones who only wanted to provide financial security. And it took me all these years to acknowledge that financial security without emotional security was all that Carter had given me, despite my mother's terrific job of providing me all the tools I needed: best schools, college fund, and even her life insurance was enough to give me a good financial head start in life.

Now, I could clearly see where Ransome and Carter differed. While Carter hounded me for an answer on taking him back, Ransome gave me space and time to clear my head and think about what I wanted.

Carter wanted me to submit to his needs without considering mine. Ransome mentioned my needs often in the few weeks I'd known him.

For the first time in my life, I was deciding what I wanted, and it felt good, liberating in a way. But it was also confusing and nerve-racking. I was just now acknowledging how much of my life I'd given up to Carter. Cooking and entertaining his friends when they wanted to come over. Going out to all of the places he picked. Living where he wanted us to live. All I had that was exclusively mine were my friends and my job.

Ransome was what my heart truly wanted, but I kept allowing my head to become filled with a river of doubt. It didn't make sense to want Ransome so badly after only having known him for a few weeks. So much could still go wrong between us. I had revealed to him that I loved him, and I think I meant it.

Did I still love Carter too? Was it possible to love two men at the same time? These were the kinds of questions and concerns that pecked at my consciousness every conceivable moment. I was so preoccupied that I didn't think to check the caller when my phone chirped. I just swiped and answered.

"Hello."

"Charla. I'm outside…"

"But I'm not…"

Click.

Carter didn't give me a chance to tell him that I wasn't ready to talk. He was intent on forcing his way back into my life, and that shit infuriated me. The worst part of my situation was that I couldn't even keep him from entering the apartment. He still had his keys.

The only reason I think he was calling was because he'd likely taken the keys off his keychain. The fact that he continued to pay for this place was also a factor we needed to rectify.

After turning the front lock open, I left a small crack in the door. I absently shuffled back to the couch, biting into my bottom lip as I stared straight ahead at nothing. I didn't have the energy to deal with him right now, but at some point, we needed to have a heart-to-heart talk.

He creaked the door open and peeked in before stepping inside. He walked up close and stood there staring down at me. When I didn't react to whatever he was doing, he plopped down on the couch next to me.

"Charla, why are you acting like this? You never used to ignore my calls. You know I want you back, baby. Why won't you let me come back home?"

I let my eyes close and was rewarded when Ransome's handsome face filled my view, causing an instant smile to form. Carter's voice sounded distant as he continued non-stop, not once asking me what I wanted or needed. He hadn't even bothered to ask the most basic question: *How was your day?*

His words faded and became background noise while images of the night Ransome had taken me to *Pure* played out in my head. My ex sat there stating his case while I recalled happier times with another man.

Ransome made me happy. He effortlessly drew the emotion from me. We didn't need to be in a long-term relationship to find happiness. The key was to try something that was better for me than the selfish man sitting next to me now.

If Ransome and I lasted another week or even a month, I believe I would gain genuine happiness from our relationship. I had gone all-in with Carter when I was still a kid and had stuck with him even when I knew deep down I wasn't happy.

He gave me the comfort that I had conveniently substituted for happiness. Since my mother had passed away a week after I graduated high school and being an only child, I believed I needed a sense of family, and I depended on Carter to fill that gap.

When you're fresh out of high school and a handsome older man with a lot going for himself gives you attention, it's easy to get sucked in. You think you see what you want in that man. You think you see the future you dreamed of. You listen to your peers when they tell you that you're lucky.

I was one of a few college freshmen who had the choice to live off campus because Carter had immediately suggested I move in with him and drive one of his cars to and from campus. By the time I graduated college, I was headed into my third year of a serious relationship.

Now, I believed I'd wasted ten years tricking myself into believing something that wasn't true, that it was a loving relationship when it had been an arrangement the entire time.

"Charla! Are you even listening?" Carter's forceful voice seemed to vibrate the couch under me. He straightened his tight, angry face when I glanced at him with an expression I'm sure was as harsh as his. I blew out a frustrated breath.

"There is no point in me listening to you. You did me a favor by walking out on me. I've had a chance to see what it's like to be happy. To know what being happy looks like."

"With that damn stripper, you've been running around with? Are you kidding me? Charla, you are a top-tier accountant for one of the most prestigious firms in this city. You don't need to lower your standards by running around with a stripper. I'm sorry I put you in a position to sink that low. And with a damn white boy too. What were you thinking?"

He talked about Ransome like he wasn't even a person. He talked about me like I didn't have enough good sense to make sound decisions for myself. I wasn't surprised that he already knew about me and Ransome. He ran a security firm and never failed to tell me how often he'd spied on me to make sure I was being a good, loyal woman. And I was stupid enough to be flattered by his spying.

I'm willing to bet he told his friends, Greg and Shawn, about *my disloyalty* the first chance he got. I had no doubt they'd filled his head with all kinds of twisted notions about me and my relationship with Ransome.

Carter's ego was so big, I believe he actually forgot that he was the one who ended our relationship, cheated on me, and got someone else pregnant. Every time I reminded myself of what *he* did, it only added fuel to my urge to strangle him.

My senses were like live wires now, allowing me to experience the full force of Carter's harsh words and the demeaning tone in which he'd spoken about Ransome. I narrowed my eyes at him, my nostrils flaring.

"His name is Ransome, and he's a person like me and you."

"And let me guess. He knows how to have fun and shows you a good time."

He shook his head and pursed his lips, adding to the glint of dissatisfaction in his eyes. I leveled a glare so fierce that he opened his mouth to speak, but his words stalled. He recovered quickly, flashing an authoritative eye in my direction. I could almost picture the speech he had lined up in his head.

"Has it ever occurred to you that showing women a good time is a stripper's job? If I left you out here astray for too long, that damn stripper would be in your bank account faster than you can bat one of your pretty little eyelashes." He lifted an exaggerated brow. "That's if he hasn't already been in it. You may as well call him and tell him to stay his ass away from you because your man is coming back home."

My head snatched back so fast at his words my neck cracked.

"Do you think that much of me? Do you think I'm so desperate that I need to pay a man for attention? Ransome has never asked me for anything except my time. I can't believe you have so little confidence in my ability to survive in this world without you."

I aimed a stiff finger at the door, my arms shaking with the anger I fought to control.

"Get the fuck out! You wanted us over, and you got it. I don't want you back."

The rainbow of emotions that flashed across his face ended in squinty-eyed anger.

"You can't put me out of here. I still pay the rent and will come and go as I damn well please. If I find that stripper was here again, I'm kicking his ass so good the hospitals will be taking bids on which facility can heal him first."

"I'll start searching for a place to stay tomorrow, so you can figure out what you want to do with this condo. Besides, you have a baby momma to take care of anyway."

I stood with my stiff finger still aimed at the door.

"Get the hell out, Carter! When you left me, I asked you to transfer the lease to my name, and you agreed that you would. Every time I tried to call you to get the paperwork done, you had excuses. Every time I tried to pay the rent, it was already paid. Every time I tried to pay you back, you returned the money. I believe your plan all along was to go see if the grass was greener, and if it wasn't, you'd have me to come back to."

His wounded-eye-stare cut through me. He made it seem like I was the unreasonable one, and he couldn't believe my behavior.

"You know what. Fuck it. I'll pack my shit and leave right now. I'll stay in a hotel before I let you hold this condo over my head."

He reached for my hand, and I yanked it away from him. He remained seated despite my request for him to leave.

"Baby, you don't have to move out. Let your man keep taking care of you like I've always done."

"Carter!" I shouted his name so loud he jumped. "What don't you understand? We are over. I'm going to pack my shit and leave, and you never have to worry about me and who I spend my time with."

He stood then. The expression on his face was one I never saw before. One part crazy, one part rage, and one part pure arrogance. However, I believe fear lingered behind the more dominant emotions.

"You're not going anywhere. You're going to stay your ass in this house, and I'm coming back home. You must be crazy if you think I'm going to let my woman continue to run around with a fucking stripper."

Carter was obviously losing his mind, and that deranged gleam in his eyes had me backing away from him.

"I'm not staying with you. If I want to run around with a stripper, that is my business. You were the one who destroyed our relationship. When I cried and begged you to come back, you practically spit in my damn face. You don't have a ring on my finger, and you can't keep me here against my will."

I flashed my naked ring finger in front of his face. He glared at my finger with a stupid smirk on his face, like he knew something that I didn't.

"I'll be back tomorrow. Call that stripper and tell him this little fling you two got going on is over."

I propped my hand up on my hip with a huff.

"I'm not doing it. As a matter of fact..." I stepped away and headed toward the bedroom, fussing to myself. "I'm packing my shit right now. I'm not staying here with you. I refuse to be your *kept* woman while you run around and do whatever the hell you want. I make good money, enough to take care of myself just fine."

I stomped into the bedroom, opening drawers as I continued to fuss to myself.

"I never checked you. Never complained. Never entertained the drama or rumors that you were cheating on me. That's the kind of woman you wanted. You wanted me as your main woman because I sat silently by while you went out and did whatever the hell you wanted."

I stepped out of the closet, dragging my suitcase. Fussing, I ran smack into Carter's hard chest. Stumbling back from the impact, I cast my wide eyes up at him.

The menacing glint in his eyes scared me. This was the first time I recalled experiencing fear around him. He stood there stalking me with his cell phone gripped tightly in his fist.

"You're going to stay your ass right here in this apartment. I'm not going to let you leave me for a damn whiteboy stripper."

An idea just occurred to me then.

"Is it Ransome's occupation or race that bothers you the most?"

Although Carter wasn't fully African-American, it didn't stop him from harboring strong biases against other races. He freely voiced his opinions, embracing some of the stereotypes and prejudices he believed were true.

He hadn't answered my question. When I moved to get closer to my dresser, he blocked my path. I shoved at his chest and attempted to sidestep him several times, but he wouldn't allow me to pass. I dropped the suitcase and ran past him, bumping his shoulder hard enough for him to stumble back.

He called after me, his voice thunderous and roaring with anger.

"I'll destroy you and that motherfucker if you leave me, Charla! I want you to listen to something. I was hoping I wouldn't have to use this to make you see reason."

His angry words stopped me in my fast-moving tracks. The sound of my voice and Ransome's coming from Carter's phone sent a chill up my spine.

My heart sputtered before it slid down to my toes. The only words that crossed my mind were, *that dirty son-of-a-bitch!*

Chapter Twenty-one

Charla

I didn't have to turn around to know that Carter had crept up behind me. My voice and Ransome's grew louder on his phone as his hot breath landed on my neck, and the first night I brought Ransome home played out vividly in my ear.

My chin fell to my chest, and my heart defied gravity and hit the floor. Carter lifted the video up to allow me to clearly see me and Ransome having sex against the dresser. My eyes slammed shut at the sight and the idea that Carter had been spying on us.

"You fucked this motherfucker, in my house, in our bedroom. You didn't think I would leave here and not keep an eye on what was happening in my own home, did you? What if I show this little recording to the Partners of Rex, Shaw, & Anders accounting firm?"

He spat his taunting words into my ear, standing so close that his comments hit me like punches.

"How about I let them see what a professional little slut, one of their top accountants, is? And don't get me started on what I'd do to your little stripper boyfriend. I'd burn down that little barbershop of his and his house. And you know I have friends in high places that would turn a blind eye even if they witnessed me doing it."

Tears dripped down my cheeks at the sound of Ransome and me having sex playing out on Carter's phone. He'd committed a crime, one he wouldn't be punished for due to those friends he'd just mentioned.

Carter and I had made a few sex videos throughout our relationship. Now that he'd revealed this recording, it had me questioning how often he recorded me through the years. Had he been keeping these types of tabs on me our entire relationship?

Security was his livelihood therefore I should have known better. A part of his business was to run surveillance and spy on people. I'd seen, first hand, the kind of damage he could do to a person with the type of information he was capable of obtaining.

"Go ahead, tell my firm," I said, sounding a lot bolder than I felt. "They know that we split up and will believe me if I tell them that you're blackmailing me because I decided to move on."

The smug bastard stood there and smiled.

"What about your little boyfriend? Are you willing to stand idly by and let me destroy his life? All you have to do is stay your ass here and work this shit out with me."

"It took me a long time to get it, Carter, but I finally did. I was hanging onto you for the convenience and the comfort you provided. I wasn't happy. I haven't been for a long time. I don't want to work it out with you. I just want to leave."

"You are not going anywhere. Is it that easy for you to throw away ten years and not try to fight to save it?"

I stared at him, unblinking. Was he crazy?

"You mean, like you did?"

"I told you, Charla. I made a fucking stupid ass mistake."

I started walking again, my steps loud and heavy. "Well, I'm not staying here, especially not with you threatening to blackmail me like I'm some kind of criminal. You say you made a stupid mistake, then you need to give me a chance to make mine."

He turned up the sound of Ransome and me having sex.

"Instead of showing your bosses this sex tape. I could bring it to the police. Tell them that the stripper followed you home, broke in, and raped you. You two did get a little rough. I can easily doctor this up to look like rape."

Those statements got my attention. I didn't miss the dare in Carter's stare, but it was the smug smile on his lips that made my anger flare. He wasn't done taunting me.

"I have no problem fixing the door and convincing my police buddies that you were too scared to tell on him. He'd go down as a rapist, and my buddies will make sure he gets taken care of once he's in prison. The corrections officers and other inmates don't take too kindly to rapists."

"What? That's crazy. You wouldn't do that. This is not you. You are not this heartless. You didn't want me a month ago. Why don't you let me go? Please," I begged, tears spilling more from anger than sorrow.

"Oh, now it's, *please*. A moment ago, you were packing your shit to go running off to that damn stripper. I'll give you twenty-four hours to call that motherfucker and tell him it's over. And don't test me, Charla. I will destroy you and him if you don't get your act together. If you know me as well as you think you do, you know I could make that fucker's life a living hell."

Ransome and me having sex continued to play out on Carter's phone, his way of beating me into complete submission. I couldn't allow him to destroy my career or Ransome's life.

I could rebuild my career, but I couldn't sit by and let him send an innocent man to jail when all Ransome wanted was to spend time with me.

I believed Carter was ruthless enough to follow through with his plan to turn Ransome into a rapist if I didn't stay with him. He assumed I was a weak, pathetic woman without him, and I'll admit, I *was* weak and for longer than I cared to admit to myself. For now, all I could do was give in to his blackmail and stay with him until I found a way to get away from him.

Blackmailed by a man I used to think loved me. How had I ended up here? You never truly know a person, no matter how much time you spend with them.

After all these years, I didn't think Carter was capable of hurting me like this. This was much worse than when he left me. I didn't blink away my thoughts until he stood snapping his finger in front of my stunned face.

"I'll be back tomorrow," he announced as he exited the bedroom. At the sound of the front door slamming shut, I staggered to the bed and sat, too stunned to do anything but stare at the walls as tears slid down my cheeks.

Carter may as well have put a gun to my head and pulled the trigger. Staying after what he threatened me with and calling it off with Ransome wasn't going to be easy. Finding a way out of this would be difficult, but my anger wouldn't allow me to give up.

After I calmed myself enough to talk, I dialed Ransome, although I knew he was probably at the club.

"Hello." His voice came across loud due to the crowd in the background. The noise level lowered after a moment, which meant he likely stepped outside or into a quieter space.

"Can we meet tomorrow at noon at the coffee shop on Howard and Lennix? I know you have to work late, so I won't keep you long."

"Sure. No problem. I'll see you there."

I hung up, unable to say more because my throat tightened, thinking of what I would have to do to him. Ransome hadn't even asked me why I picked such a random place. It was one of the reasons I liked him. If it made me smile, he was all for it.

I chose that coffee shop because I knew Carter hated coffee, and it was nowhere near either of our places of employment. I didn't want to take the chance of Carter being able to spy on me. I also had to consider that he was crazy enough to have someone follow me.

No longer able to form complete sentences. I couldn't call Dayton or Callie. They would hear the cracks in my voice and race over. They would start a fight with Carter on my behalf, and he would end up saying or doing something to hurt them. I couldn't allow them to get hurt due to my mess. For now, I was on my own.

Eventually, I would have to tell my friends I was taking Carter back. I didn't know yet if I was telling them the *why* behind the decision.

Chapter Twenty-two

Charla

My hand shook against the mug of coffee I had no intention of drinking. Now that my thoughts were flowing again, I remembered mentioning to Ransome that I rarely drank coffee, and neither did he. Yet, he was on his way to meet me anyway.

I arrived early enough to wrangle my raging thoughts and find a way to tell a man I cared about deeply that I didn't want to see him anymore. Why hadn't I taken the coward's way out and done this over the phone?

The moment Ransome stepped up to the entrance door and walked into the building, his eyes found me, and his smile lit up his face.

I would miss those radiantly beautiful eyes. I would miss his soft warm lips on mine and everywhere on me. The way he took control of my body and made me feel so good. The way he made me come every time. The way his strong hands slid so delicately along every line and curve of my body. The way he stared so intently into my eyes and ran his gaze over me like I was the only woman in his world.

Ransome's smile encouraged mine to surface, although I had nothing to smile about. His smile dropped when he got a good look at my face. There was no way to hid that I'd been crying. He reached and took my trembling hand, and I let him.

"What's wrong? What can I do?"

"We can't see each other anymore," I blurted. I can't believe I'd gotten it out. I didn't want to prolong this. So there. I'd said the words that had my heart splintering in my chest. Ransome didn't let my hand go after those words, and I noticed I hadn't let go of his either.

"You've decided to take *him* back?"

I couldn't reply through the knots of sorrow clogging my throat. Tears fell, and my broken heart spilled a river of blood. I nodded, making the tears dropped faster. Ransome reached out and wiped tears from my eyes.

"You don't seem happy about your decision."

I couldn't say anything because he was right. I was forced into my decision. It was because of me that he could end up labeled a rapist and end up in prison, where Carter's buddies could ruin his life further. I had to do this. I had to let him go.

Ransome sat, silently assessing me like he sensed that something was off. I was supposed to act like a bitch so he would hate me, but I couldn't bring myself to treat him badly. I was doing enough by breaking it off with him.

"If you need me, call me, Charlene. Anytime. Okay." My head shook absently. The adoration in his eyes in the face of what was happening between us broke me down even further.

Ransome stood and pulled his hand from my tight grip. He stepped around the table and stood above me before he took a knee next to me.

"Are you sure you're okay?"

"I'm okay. Thank you," I choked out before more tears leaked, and my throat tightened into a constricting knot.

Ransome brushed a tender kiss across my cheek and let his lips linger at my ear.

"I love you, Charlene," he whispered.

I closed my eyes and didn't open them until his warmth left my side. He still loved me even after I broke things off with him—after I broke his heart. He had no idea, but I'd also broken my own heart. I loved Ransome. I loved him more than he would ever know.

The act of letting him go had broken me mentally, and it was only a matter of time before it affected me physically. Carter claimed he wanted me, but what he would receive may make him change his mind. I wasn't the same Charla he believed he knew.

***

I returned to the office and buried myself in work. I stayed until Carter called me around eight p.m. I informed him that I was working on a big project, which wasn't a total lie, and stayed there for another hour.

When I walked into the apartment, he was sitting on the couch with a glass of scotch in his hand. I didn't bother greeting him. I headed straight to the guest bedroom, where I'd moved most of my clothes, and locked myself inside.

***

Thankfully, Carter didn't bother me for the first week, but after a week of my mean looks, sexless nights, and silent treatment, I believed he'd had enough.

I shove my key into the front door lock, regretfully turned the knob, and frown at the sight of Carter standing from the couch when I stepped inside. I released a frustrated sigh

"Why won't you talk to me, Charla? By now, you should at least understand I did this to protect you. To keep you from making a mistake."

My eyes rolled so hard that the act left a slight ache in my temples. I took off so fast that his head jerked back at my sudden movement. I stormed past him and slammed the guest bedroom door in his face.

What the hell did he expect? Me to forgive and forget about him recording me and threatening to ruin me and an innocent man's life?

The next night, he sat on the couch staring like he usually did when I strolled into the house after a long workday. With all the hours of free overtime I was putting in, the firm was benefiting nicely from my personal situation. I could hear Carter shuffling behind me as I made my way to the guest bedroom.

"Talk to me, Charla," he called after me.

"Why the fuck would I want to talk to you? You're blackmailing me to stay with you when it's clear I don't want to be with you anymore."

He closed the distance between us so fast, I gasped when he spun me and stood there in my face. He reached down to take my hand, and I slapped his hand away so hard that the sting radiated through my palm.

"Don't fucking touch me. How could you believe that I would want to be with you again?"

A deep chuckle fell from my throat, a sound I didn't even recognize coming from myself. "Maybe you can blackmail me into having sex with you since you're so good at blackmailing people. If sex is what you want, you're going to have to take it."

My sharp words caused his head to snap back.

"I can't believe you'd say some shit like that to me. You know I'm not going to rape you."

"You already have. You raped me repeatedly with a nail-spiked dick the night you blackmailed me into staying with you. I never thought you'd be the person to hurt me this badly."

His mouth opened and closed a few times, but he couldn't spit his words out. I'd never talked to him this way.

I stepped into the bedroom and prayed he wasn't following me. The idea made me turn and level a glare at Carter with so much disdain he swallowed hard and took a step back. He stood in my doorway looking at me and appeared to be at a loss for words. When I reached for the door handle, his eyes tracked my movements before I slammed the door so hard that tiny pieces of wood chips flew away from it.

Chapter Twenty-three

Ransome

Atlas and Trent sat across the table, talking about their newest flings. My thoughts, on the other hand, were on one woman, Charlene.

She was everything any man could ever want in a woman. Smart, beautiful, thoughtful, hardworking. And the sex—my God. Thinking about the way she made me feel had my skin tingling. The way her soft lips would glide against mine, teasing my neck and massaging my dick.

Trent snapped his fingers in front of my face.

"Earth to Ransome, earth to Ransome. Ransome, you there?"

I snapped out of my head to see what he wanted. He pointed at a table near the bar.

"Aren't they your girlfriend's friends? Kind of hard to forget a group of women that damn fine."

I sat up, stretching my neck to see over the busy lunchtime crowd. It was Callie and Dayton. They waved when they noticed me. I returned their wave and glanced back at my friends, who eyeballed me suspiciously.

"Aren't you going to invite them to sit with us? Just because their friend dumped you doesn't mean you need to blackball the rest of us," Atlas said, his eyes boring into me.

"Hell no! Not so you two hounds could sink your teeth into them."

Telling those two that Charla had dumped me had been a mistake. I was teased and taunted for the last couple of weeks about how I couldn't handle a woman of

Charla's caliber. She was out of my league. Stripping wasn't going to cut it. I didn't make enough money. They had said it all, and as much as I hated to think it, I wondered, were they right? Was I not financially secure enough for her? Did she think that I was too immature, not accomplished enough?

"Come on, man. They're hot. And not cheesy or slutty hot either. They are classy and hot, like that friend that dumped you. I have to admit, if you have to get dumped, it may as well be by a classy ass hot chick like that," Atlas said, his eyeballs sparking with intrigue. He pleaded with his eyes, begging me to invite the ladies to our booth.

Usually, Trent, the true player of our group, was the one who was always eager to link up with hot women. Instead, it was Atlas advocating to get some face time with Charla's friends. Atlas was usually the secret rendezvous type who only told us about his flings when they ended.

I stood, and Atlas smiled. When I picked up my plate, he stared, dumbstruck for a second. Trent appeared distracted, his eyes unfocused, his stare fixed on nothing. He was likely thinking about his next hookup.

"Excuse me, gentlemen."

"You ass," Atlas hissed. The comment was hurled at my back as I stepped away from our table and headed toward the ladies.

Surprisingly warm smiles greeted me as I made my approach.

"Ladies, if you don't mind. May I please join you."

The one I knew as Callie inclined her head and slid over on her side of their booth. Dayton smiled and glanced back at my friends, who broke their necks, staring at us.

"Your friends are going to hurt themselves over there," Dayton commented.

"How's Charlene?" I asked, desperate for any update on her.

Callie eyed me suspiciously. Dayton leaned across the table with an accusatory glance.

"Shit. I was hoping you could tell us. She called, saying she was taking that asshole back. And now, she's been avoiding our calls. What did you do to her?"

My glum expression removed the sting from both their eyes.

"I didn't do anything. She called me one day, invited me for coffee, and before I could get comfortable in my seat, she told me she didn't want to see me anymore. That she was taking her ex back."

"Fuck!" Dayton snapped. "Why the fuck would she want that rat bastard back? I don't like your job, but you were doing something right because she was *happy*. I mean, her whole spirit was lifted, and she was smiling like I'd never seen her with Carter's punk ass."

I suppose her statement could qualify as a compliment. And I would venture to say that Dayton didn't like Carter. She expressly didn't like Charla being with him. Based on the tight pull at the corners of her mouth and the deep frown on her face, she would have been happy with a serial killer for her friend versus Carter.

Callie chimed in. "She hasn't been acting like herself for the last few weeks. She won't even have lunch with us. It almost feels like she's hiding."

Callie shrugged, her eyes aimed at my chest while she worked out the logic of the situation in her head.

"I believe she's ashamed of herself for taking Carter back. I mean…" Dayton cut off her own words and glanced at me, unwilling to divulge too much of her friend's business.

"She said he cheated on her and got someone else pregnant," I told them so they would know that Charla and I had shared a lot more than bodily fluids.

Dayton's eyebrows shot up. "She told you that?"

"Yes. She also said they'd been together going on ten years. I guess the amount of time they had together won out over happiness."

"Why would she go back to him?" Callie asked absently. "She's obviously not happy with him. She's avoiding our calls and dodging our lunch dates. Hell, she didn't even participate in our spa time this week. Something is wrong. You don't think Carter is bullying her?"

The question lifted my brows and Dayton's hackles.

"He better not be. He's already robbed her of years that she could have been happy with someone else," Dayton muttered.

Dayton aimed her finger between her and Callie. "We'll get to the bottom of this shit. If that cheating bastard is being an asshole to our friend, I'll find a way to make him pay."

I had no idea if what Charla's friends said held any relevance, but it would explain her dumping me so abruptly for no reason.

"Is there anything I can do? I want Charla to be happy, even if it's not with me."

My comment drew a smile from their faces, but Dayton answered. "You hang tight, Mr. Stripper Man. If there is a bottom to get to, you best believe we're going to find it."

I nodded, but my attention was drawn to the sight of Trent and Atlas strolling up.

"Mind if we join you ladies?" Atlas asked.

"Sure," Dayton answered with a huge smile plastered on her face. On the other hand, Callie appeared conflicted, especially when Trent's gaze met hers across the table.

Trent and Atlas sat next to Dayton at her side of the booth, and I remained next to Callie. Trent's eyes went straight to Callie, and Atlas sat in the middle next to Dayton.

A cordial conversation kept us going, but after some time, I noticed Atlas, who advocated for a seat at this table, now appeared uncomfortable. Dayton sat next to him with a similar vibe like they were fighting not to touch each other. She even inched closer to the wall to put a little distance between them.

"That is a lovely dress you're wearing," Atlas finally spoke up, complementing Callie. She perked up, her smile resurfacing.

"I made it myself," she said proudly. She and Atlas launched into a conversation about, of all things, fashion.

Tense shoulders and a deep crease lined Trent's forehead. Trent was upset all of a sudden. Was Callie the one he was interested in, and he didn't like Atlas talking to her?

Was I reading too much into the weird exchanges taking place at this table? I didn't know what I was seeing. It didn't matter because thoughts of Charla consumed me so thoroughly, everything around me faded into the background.

Chapter Twenty-four

Charla

I parked Dayton's black Acura inside the parking garage of the hotel so no one would see me exiting it from the street or see me going into the hotel. I lied to Dayton about my car being in the shop, so being the true friend that she is, she made a plan to carpool home from work with her co-workers and let me use her car for a few hours.

Three minutes later, the elevator still hadn't arrived. I checked my personal emails on my phone and scanned my only two social media accounts to make sure Carter hadn't done anything crazy, like leaking my sex tape that he'd illegally recorded.

Hidden behind tons of concrete inside this garage, I still felt vulnerable to Carter's spying eyes. I knew the man couldn't be everywhere at once, but I was paranoid that he had eyes on me nonetheless. Hopefully, if he did have someone following me, my driving Dayton's car would have thrown the person off.

At this point, I didn't know what my ex was capable of or what lengths he would go to punish me or keep me. I couldn't figure out what it was he wanted from me. He spent years taking me for granted, and I foolishly let him. Now he believed he was entitled to me, no matter his actions.

Dayton and Callie were a part of the reason I was meeting the out-of-state private investigator, Douglas Roberts, whom I hired. I needed to find dirt equally as damaging as the dirt Carter had on me before things between us got any worse.

Carter's devious behavior had aided in turning me into one of those women who spent their spare time spying and plotting. I was a woman scorned in more ways than I could count at this point. Over the course of the past few weeks, when I wasn't working, I was doing everything I could to dig up dirt on Carter.

My objective with the detective was to see if I could find enough dirt to counteract the threats Carter made against me and Ransome. Mr. Roberts was a well-preserved sixty-year-old who had come highly recommended by a trusted co-worker who used him to spy on her cheating husband.

His hair was snow white, but his skin was wrinkle-free with a freshness to it that gave him a youthful appearance. He reminded me of Anderson Cooper. His resume stated that he'd spent twenty years in the Marines and another twenty as an Atlanta detective.

So far, he was providing answers to some of the suspicions I had about Carter, like the fact that he was leasing a secret apartment. But that wasn't all. Carter was also sleeping with another of his mistresses, who happened to be married. It wasn't that she was married—it was who she was married to that rang alarm bells. Maxine Wells was the wife of our City Councilman, Lawrence Wells. It would be interesting to see how the conservative City Councilman would react knowing the wife he often put on a pedestal was sleeping with a black man. Wells had come under scrutiny for several racism lawsuits filed against him a few years back but had avoided the courts and settled both cases quickly.

Based on news reports, Lawrence Wells' wife was the love of his life. The updates Mr. Roberts fed me made me question what else Carter had been getting into right under my nose. That's why he wanted to keep me. I had ignored his dirty deeds for nearly a decade.

The revelation about him screwing the Councilman's wife was juicy, but I believed I needed more to make Carter heel like the low-down, flea ridden dog he was.

Finishing up our conversation, my attention was drawn to a vision I never expected to see again. The handsome face of Ransome.

Was I seeing things now? I blinked hard to make sure I wasn't daydreaming since Ransome was on my mind so often. My heart had been broken, but had the rest of me been broken as well?

"Are you okay, Ms. McGregor?" Mr. Roberts asked, concern creasing his forehead.

I snapped out of my haze to find Ransome continuing to fill my view as he walked toward the hotel lobby bar where I'd decided to meet Mr. Roberts.

The idea that I would see him in a hotel I'd picked at random had me thinking about a conversation we'd had during one of our late-night chats about fate and timing.

"I'm okay, Mr. Roberts. Let me know when you find anything else."

I shook the hand he held out to me before he walked away. As soon as Mr. Roberts disappeared through the shiny gold and black revolving doors, my gaze immediately traveled to the area where I had spotted Ransome.

And there he was, walking my way in blue joggers, a plain white T-shirt and tennis shoes. Dressed down, the man dripped sex appeal so fluidly that he demanded attention without even trying. My memories of him kept me from losing my mind while being trapped in that apartment with Carter for the past three and a half weeks.

He pointed at the chair Mr. Roberts had vacated.

"May I?"

"Yes," I whispered the word, awed by his presence.

I was happy to see him but terrified of Carter finding out I was this close to him. Nervously, I glanced around the hotel lobby, my eyes darting in every direction. Although none of Carter's security guards worked here, I was still on edge.

The last thing I needed was the crazy asshole blowing up our lives. Now that Ransome was here, my sneaking around had taken on a whole other definition.

Chapter Twenty-five

Ransome

Seeing Charla again after weeks of no contact had thawed my ice-capped heart and set it to thumping out new dance moves in my chest. She was all I'd been thinking about since she'd dumped me. It had taken every damn muscle in my body not to reach for my phone and check on her.

I had driven by her apartment complex three times, but common sense kept me from driving up to the gate and entering the code. I also reminded myself that I wasn't a stalker.

Charla visited me in my dreams every night and in my daydreams during the day. I messed up my first haircut last week because I couldn't concentrate long enough to focus on what the hell I was doing. Thankfully, the customer was a young kid who opted to let me give him a low fade versus the cut he asked for after I offered him free cuts for two months.

Now, here she was in the flesh. Charlene McGregor. The woman who'd stolen my heart. She hadn't even bothered to return it when she decided to take her ex-boyfriend back.

The same way I had spotted her in that dim club the night I met her, my eyes found Charlene walking inside the lobby of a hotel at the well-timed opening of the front doors. My vision had zoomed clear across a crowded street of walking pedestrians and moving vehicles.

Atlas and Trent looked at me like I'd lost my damn mind when I slung my gym bag at them and took off across the busy intersection. Heck, I didn't even know if they understood me when I yelled back that I would catch up to them later.

After spotting Charla, I posted up in a corner inside the hotel lobby to confirm that my eyes weren't playing tricks on me. Once I knew that it was her, I spied on her sitting at a table in the lobby restaurant, talking to an older man.

She was in a gray and pink skirt suit and appeared to be discussing business. He must have been one of the clients from her accounting firm. If so, why had they decided to meet on the opposite side of the city?

When I could no longer take the mystery or stifle my urge to be closer to her, I walked into the bar and waited for her to finish her conversation. For a second, our eyes locked and the penetrating force from the connection felt like being kicked in the chest.

Staring at her even at a distance made my heart speed up and I took deep breaths to calm my raging emotions. She wasn't upset by my presence. Surprise appeared to be the emotion that dominated her features, distracting her enough for the man sitting in front of her to wave a hand in front of her face to recapture her attention.

She continued her conversation with the man while sending occasional glances in my direction. As soon as the man walked away, I headed in her direction, praying during my walk that she would at least talk to me.

I aimed a pleading finger at the seat in front of her. "May I?"

She nodded and gave me a quick, "Yes" while glancing around like she was expecting someone else. Her head was on a constant swivel, darting around the lobby as she shifted in her seat.

Although stressed, she was still the most beautiful woman I'd ever laid eyes on. What was going on to have her so distracted?

"I'm not stalking you if that's what you're thinking," I stated in an attempt to ease some of her radiating tension. "One of the gyms I go to with the guys is a few blocks from here."

"I didn't think that you were stalking me. I'm just surprised to see you."

Her eyes darted around again like she would get into trouble for being near me. Could her friends have been right in their assumption about her ex-boyfriend? Was he bullying her into staying with him?

The scenario didn't make sense. Charla wasn't the type of woman who would allow herself to be bullied.

"Are you okay? You are beautiful as always, but you look…stressed."

Her eyes dropped, and her shoulders slumped a little.

"I'm okay. Just having a difficult time dealing with…something."

Shit!

I tensed at the sight of tears forming in her eyes. When the tiny droplets pooled at the corners of her eyes and slid down her cheeks, I rose from my chair and reached for her hand.

She hesitated, staring at my outstretched hand before reaching out and allowing me to take hers. I tugged her up from her seat.

"Come with me. We need to talk. In private."

"We shouldn't be talking at all," she said, attempting to assert emotional distance. But it didn't work. There was no authority or enough edge in her tone to even consider her words.

I gripped her hand tighter, tugged, and waltzed her straight to the ladies' room. She didn't give any resisting actions or words but simply allowed me to escort her to a place where we could talk without eyes and ears on us.

Once we stepped inside the small space that was meant for individual use, I reached around Charla's body and locked us inside. We stood so close her sweet fragrance drifted up my flaring nostrils. The warmth of her skin radiated into mine.

I couldn't resist cupping her face and tilting her head up so that our eyes could meet.

"Charla, what's wrong? And don't tell me it's nothing. I meant it when I told you to call me if you needed me. I'll do whatever you need me to do."

Her forehead tensed and released several times while her eyes searched my face. I had no doubt she found the truth of my words in my set features.

"I can't be here with you. We aren't together anymore. I need to get back to work."

Her words sounded forced and mechanical like she had practiced them. She attempted to walk away, but I placed my hands on either side of her body and leaned my face close to hers, not giving her a choice but to glance into my eyes.

I had no idea if someone could tell by a look if you loved them or not, but I'm sure my emotions for Charla were written in my body language and pouring from my eyes.

My forehead creased when I saw what I was feeling reflected back at me in her watery gaze. Charla loved me. There was nothing she could say that would convince me to ignore what I felt, what I sensed, what I knew.

I honestly don't know what happened to the talk we were supposed to be having. My words, and I believe hers, as well, were being burned away by the sudden flow of our hot passion. Our lips gravitated toward each other, and when they touched, fireworks.

My lips were on hers, and she kissed me back with as much passion. This woman had the power to make me lose my damn mind. All hope of being sensible was gone now.

When I deepened our kiss, her soft moan against my lips set off sparks of lust that shot straight to my groin. I gathered her gray knee-length skirt and lifted it before I lifted her. Her legs were up and locked around my waist as our tongues reunited.

Charla wasn't my woman. She'd chosen her ex, but there was nothing I could do to make myself not want her. It was impossible. I couldn't undo the love I'd developed for her. The insatiable want. The burning need. My inability to let her go had landed us here, in this bathroom, about to commit to a forbidden act.

My hand slid up her silky legs as I ground my pelvis into her. She did nothing to stop me. Instead, she encouraged me with her sensual movements. The way her body was flowing against mine, and she was telling me, loud and clear, how badly she missed and wanted me.

Our desperate hands. Our heated moans into each other's mouths. We were reaching a point of no return.

I pulled back and stopped all movement, attempting to dampen my behavior. Charla's eyes reflected pure uncut lust and begging desire.

Our harsh breathing echoed off the marble-white walls and filled the space of the bathroom. We stared into each other's eyes, communicating a message that we fully understood but, at the same time, didn't. Her hands were at my waist, inching my shirt up so she could caress my bare skin.

With her pinned between the wall and me, I reached down with one hand and shoved my sweat shorts down my legs enough to free myself. Her hiked-up skirt was bunched around her waist, exposing sheer blue panties. It took little effort to slide the thin material to the side.

"You're so wet for me, baby," I breathed into her mouth while running my finger over her wet heat.

My words bounced off her cheek as I traced her hot, quivering core with my finger. Her response to my statement was the tender kiss she placed on my warm trembling lips.

The things Charla had the ability to make me feel couldn't be described. It was like being connected to a live wire that fed pleasure, pain, love, lust, and every other emotion I could name into every inch of me.

Our lips fell open, and a harsh intake of air filled our lungs when I plunged my dick into her warm and drenched pussy. I drew back slightly and repeated the action, unable to stop giving what she desperately received.

"Ransome," she called out against my ear in a sweet, lusty tone that fueled my urge to push into her harder. Her nails sank into my shoulder and back where she held onto me. Words weren't necessary because there weren't any that could explain us and our connection.

Our bodies did all the talking as we clung, twirled, twisted, pumped, and ground ourselves into each other. We feasted until the dam of desire we'd built broke.

We remained connected to each other for a hot, heaving minute. I didn't loosen my grip on Charla until my mind returned and reclaimed me.

Charla loosened her legs, and I let her body slide down the wall until she landed back safely on her feet. She fixed her skirt with shaky hands and downcast eyes, and I stuffed my dick back inside my pants. I reached down to help her get back into one of those sexy black pumps that had fallen off her feet during our moment of intensely hot public bathroom sex.

Speechless at this point, I didn't know what to say. I had brought her into this bathroom to talk. To figure out what was wrong with her. To help her. Instead, I'd helped myself to a hearty helping of her delicious body. I got the impression she needed our physical connection more than she wanted to discuss her problems.

"Ransome," she breathed out harshly. "We can't do this again. I have to go."

"But we still need to talk," I stated, still winded and feeling the effects of the high she'd gifted me with.

She fumbled with the door and ran out of the bathroom like it had caught fire.

"But. But. Wait!"

Charla loved me. I had no doubt about what we shared. So, why was she running, and the even bigger question, why was she still with her damn ex? Something was going on.

By the time I made it into the lobby, she had disappeared. I stared around the place, lost, as people eyeballed me with suspicious gazes.

Chapter Twenty-six

Charla

The well of tears threatening to roll down my cheeks was telling little reminders of the pain I suffered for having to let Ransome go—again. The only time I wasn't fighting back tears lately was when I was at work, plunging myself into my workload.

I needed the distraction for two reasons. One, to stave off my desire to run back to Ransome. And two, to keep myself from slapping the piss out of Carter.

Why the hell was Carter talking to me right now? His ear-grating voice had greeted me, when I walked into the condo five minutes ago. Reluctantly, I'd taken a seat on the couch, not because I was interested in what he had to say, but because my damn feet hurt.

I half listened to his chatter, vaguely understanding the words pouring from his mouth. Sucking in a deep breath, I held it before I let my eyes roll into the top of my head.

I toed off my leather platform pumps and fought the desperate urge to hurl them at Carter's face. Hopefully, they would hit him in his mouth to shut him the hell up.

There was nothing he could say or do at this point that would ever make me forgive him. He'd had all the time in the world to do right by me, and based on his history, I doubted he had the capacity and discipline to even know what right meant.

Why didn't he just let me go?

His ego.

Carter's ego had led us here. After he'd seen me having sex with Ransome, it must have driven him over the edge. And even worse, if he'd been recording us the whole time, he'd likely seen us having sex repeatedly in every imaginable position.

I'm sure he also *enjoyed* our tender and playful moments. Ransome had given me the kind of attention that I craved but had long stopped trying to get from Carter.

It had been five days since mine and Ransome's hot bathroom scene, one I couldn't get out of my head. Carter hadn't mentioned anything, and nothing about his body language suggested he was upset. It was safe to assume he didn't have any spies who'd followed me to that hotel.

"Charla, I wasn't trying to hurt you. I did this to keep you from making a mistake you'll regret later."

"Like the mistakes you repeatedly made."

My snappy comment finally got his lips to stop flapping. I lifted my hand so that I could start my count.

"Let's see. You cheated on me multiple times. While cheating, you were having unprotected sex and bringing your raw, potentially diseased dick back to me. What about the mistake you made when you left me?"

I shook an accusatory finger at him.

"You threw me away like I was a piece of trash. Then, you came back into this house, treating me like a criminal because of a situation *you* created. Oh, let's not forget you illegally recorded me and used the recording to threaten me and an unsuspecting man's livelihood."

I took a deep breath and closed my eyes to rein in the strength I needed to keep from flying off into a cursing fit. Now, I finally understood how women could snap and use physical violence. At this point, being trapped with a man I despised had my nerves so on edge. Every time he came near me, I clenched my fist, desperately fighting the burning rage curling inside that urged me to dispense physical pain.

I wasn't a fighter, but Carter had pushed me to my limits, and dragging this torture out was driving me to the edge of my sanity. I had never cursed so much in my life as I'd cursed at Carter during the last month.

He went quiet after I called out some of his mistakes. He stood and paced with his head lowered like he was working something out in his head.

"You broke my heart for the first time when you walked out on me. Time allowed it to heal. Then you came right back in here and broke it again when you threatened to ruin my life."

I kept calling out his mistakes, knowing it was the last things he wanted to hear.

I stood abruptly before advancing toward him. The hate in my gaze must have been severe because it made his body stiffen like he expected me to hit him.

"I hate you, Timothy Carter."

I spit the words at him so viciously, he took a step back like I'd thrown blows.

"I'm sorry, Charla. I didn't…"

"Can I leave then?" I cut him off. "If you're so fucking sorry like you keep saying. Can I go?"

His head shook slowly, his eyes squinting at the corners.

"No, because you'll likely go running to *him,* and I'll be forced to destroy him. I know you don't want that on your conscience."

He was still being a major dick. He just couldn't take the loss. I didn't respond to his threats or his guilt-evoking words. He operated under the mentality that if he couldn't have me, he wasn't going to allow anyone else to have me, either.

He continued to talk, and I continued to not listen while stepping away so that his words would bounce off my back. I had a meeting with Mr. Roberts tomorrow and prayed he found something strong enough for me to put Carter in his place.

Carter followed me as I headed toward my bedroom, his irritating voice grating on my last damn nerve. I went on about the business of gathering my clothes for a shower as he talked to himself because I damn sure wasn't listening.

This was another of his countless attempts to convince me that his twisted side of the situation was the right side. How much longer would it take him to figure out that nothing he said would make me listen or want him? Nothing he said or did would make me forgive him. All Timothy Carter could do at this point was let me go.

"Charla! Would you look at me, please?!"

His raised voice indicated that he was getting pissed off at my dismissive behavior. I wasn't sure how long he'd been trying to get my attention either. I did notice that he'd been reduced to using the word, *please.*

After I closed my drawer, I tucked my clothes under my arm before I turned to face him. My deadly gaze raked over him from top to bottom before I let my eyes keep rolling upward.

How could I have ever loved this man? What kind of spell had I been under?

The death of my mother shouldn't have been the reason I accepted a man like Carter into my life, but I believe it was. I believe grief was what blinded me to who Carter truly was. He'd come along when my heart was so broken that I would have accepted anyone to make the hurt go away.

My mother had been my best friend. We got along like sisters. When she died, I truly believed a part of me had gone with her.

Carter had gone deathly still wearing a pinched expression. The tension around his eyes tightened. I believed he was experiencing a loss for words since he wasn't used to me being so hostile. One of my eyebrows lifted as I took him in. When he lowered to the floor, dropping to one knee, I choked down the loud outburst of laughter that threatened to come out.

He was on the floor with a little blue box in his hands. It took a serious amount of effort to keep my laughter from springing into action because it would assuredly set him off in a bad way. My lips puckered into a tight knot, and when that didn't work, I clamped my teeth into my bottom lip.

"Charla. Will you marry me? I love you. I can't live without you in my life."

The laughter broke free despite my efforts to stop it. I cackled, hee-hee'd, and ha-hawed with chest-shaking gusto. This was the funniest thing I'd seen and heard in years.

I even pointed down at him with one hand as my other sat atop my quaking stomach. I literally laughed until my stomach and chest hurt, bending at the waist to relieve some of the pressure.

Carter sprang up from the floor, snapping the box shut. He glared at me, fuming, his chest lifting and falling fast and hard. If the heat flaring off of his body could burn, I would have been in flames.

The man must have lost his natural mind if he believed I was marrying him. Even if he hadn't blackmailed me into staying with him, even if I hadn't found out about his married mistress, he still had a girlfriend that he'd gotten pregnant while with me.

My laughter at his proposal cut him deep. He puffed up his chest and got in my face like he was about to hit me. When I didn't back away and stared him in the eyes, he spun away and stormed out of my bedroom, cursing his ass off.

"Motherfucking women. Don't appreciate a good man. I fucking try to do the right thing, and look what it gets me. I got something for her ass. I don't need this shit."

He slammed the bedroom door so hard it jumped the lock, sprang back open, and hit the wall. The paneling around the edges splintered, and the doorknob wobbled in its housing.

The sight of the broken door made me laugh even harder. I think perhaps I was losing my mind right along with Carter.

I couldn't understand why he wanted me so badly after he'd so easily tossed me away. He'd had ten years to prove how much he wanted and appreciated me. Now, nothing he did or said would ever make me believe he'd changed.

Chapter Twenty-seven

Ransome

"I'm not crazy," I kept chanting the phrase to myself while hunkering low in the shadows and peering through the glass and into the building at the person I was spying on inside.

There was no other explanation for my actions other than I loved Charlene. I'd allowed myself to fall deep, hard, and fast. Now, I didn't know how to control these overwhelming urges. I had to protect her, even if I didn't know what I was protecting her from.

I'd always heard people say love can make a person do some crazy shit, but I never believed it until now. I eased back, allowing the darkness surrounding the area to swallow me when Carter approached the door to exit the building. He'd been inside talking to his night security crew, who worked the lobby of the Max-Fletcher building that housed law offices.

Based on his angry finger-pointing and aggressive body posture toward the two men sitting behind the counter, it was safe to say he'd just cursed the men out. As soon as he turned his back to the men, their angry sneers followed him out the glass doors.

My encounter with Charlene in that bathroom kept playing on a loop in my head. She still wanted me. She still had feelings for me. I felt it, and I know she did too.

Now, I couldn't shake the sick feeling that Carter was forcing or bullying her into staying with him. Since the night I saw him exiting Charla's apartment with anger dripping off him like water, I sensed that something was off. I stalked his social media feeds and read everything posted publicly about him and his security company.

Tonight, around six, by some twisted chance of fate, I'd spotted Carter coming out of one of the many buildings that lined this street. It was after eight now, and I was still spying on him.

He'd been making his rounds, checking out the work sites his men secured. I didn't know what I was looking for, but I discovered from watching him that Carter was a world-class asshole to nearly everyone he encountered. He treated his employees like shit. He bumped into people, knocking them out of his way like he owned the city.

He was heading back to his car now after illegally parking it outside the parking garage of the building he was stepping out of. I had to confront him. I had to say something. But what? What if my approaching Carter made things worse for Charlene? How could I help her when she wouldn't talk to me and tell me what was wrong?

"Fuck," I muttered under my breath the closer he came to my location. The area was open to pedestrians, but they avoided it due to the scaffolding and construction equipment built to form a tunnel over the walkway.

Thanks to the equipment, the streetlights didn't provide adequate lighting to the area, leaving a long stretch of it drenched in shadows.

"Yeah," Carter said, the light against his face indicating he was on his phone. He kept walking until he was under the tunnel of masonry equipment.

"Slow down. What?" he said, his voice carrying under the makeshift tunnel so that I heard him loud and clear.

"Baby, you need to calm down. It's perfectly normal," he said, concern heavy in his tone.

Was something wrong with Charlene? I crept closer to him, listening to his side of the conversation but stupidly wanting to get closer to Charlene, even if just to hear the sound of her voice to make sure she was okay.

"Nicola, I told you that I was coming over. Now watch some television or something until I finish making my rounds."

At the sound of him calling out another woman's name, my whole demeanor shifted. The asshole wasn't even talking to Charlene. It was probably the woman he'd left Charlene for, the one he'd broken Charla's heart over when he left her. He'd somehow convinced Charlene to take him back but was standing here vocally consoling his other woman and promising her that he was coming over.

What about Charlene? Didn't she deserve a faithful man? One who would put her needs before his own. One who wouldn't take her for granted. One who would do anything to make her happy. Carter was not that man.

Rage, blinding and quick, filled me. The idea that I was being too erratic and crazy went out the window. I had to do something, and I wasn't altogether sure if I or Carter would be okay when I was done.

Chapter Twenty-eight

Charla

The next day.

What the hell happened to his face? Carter had gotten into a fight, and based on the fake sorrow flashing in his eyes, he was itching for me to ask what happened, to care and show concern.

I sat in the chair while he was on the couch, watching me ignore him and not respond to his attempts to engage in conversation. I didn't ask after him, and I believed it was eating his ass alive.

He huffed and puffed and kept touching his busted lip. The sight of his swollen right eye and the bruises on his face and neck forced me to fight back a smile.

I hope the person he fought didn't have a scratch on them. I'd even go as far as kissing the person if I met them. Carter had done a lot of people wrong, so his run-in could have been with anyone.

"I was mugged, in case you're wondering what happened to me. Two assholes jumped me in front of the Max-Fletcher building when I was on my way back to my car last night," he volunteered, tired of waiting for me to ask. His words had broken the tense silence filling up the space.

"I actually wasn't wondering. That's your business," I said, the sarcasm in my tone thick and precise.

He pursed his lips and shook his head but didn't reply to my biting comments. He released another long sigh before squeezing his forehead, his eyes fixed on me the whole time. It was killing him that he couldn't make me bend to his will like he once could.

If he was going for intimidation with his staring, it wasn't working, especially with his face looking like he'd banged it into a brick wall.

"I need to go to one of the work sites. I'll be back soon," he said like I gave a shit. I didn't care where he went and prayed he didn't come back. He cast a lingering glance back that I couldn't read before pulling the door closed behind him.

Carter had been attempting to talk to me since I arrived home from work an hour ago, but the most he'd gotten from me was teeth-sucking and rolling eyes. The last thing I wanted to see after working all day was him.

I wasn't as stupid as Carter assumed. His little announcement was nothing more than code for him going to check on his baby momma.

"Think about something else," I whispered to myself, closing my eyes to manifest positive thoughts. There must be a way to get away from Carter without mine and Ransome's lives getting ruined. I prayed that the investigator found some blackmail worthy dirt on Carter because I refused to be trapped in a relationship I now despised.

Tears began to pool in my eyes out of nowhere, reminding me of the emotional turmoil of this situation.

I'd let myself be Carter's little follower for so long that I never imagined having to think myself out of this fucked up situation I allowed him to box me into. My girls would gladly help, but I didn't need Carter adding them to his hit list.

Dayton had already called and interrogated me twice, especially when I asked to use her car and blatantly lied about mine being in the shop. Callie called, texted, and babied me over the phone like I'd been abducted by the devil.

The notion of *working it out* with Carter was laughable. I didn't want to work shit out with him except which hospital he wanted to be admitted to after I bashed him across his skull with something hard and heavy.

I jumped. The sound of someone aggressively ringing my doorbell and the consistent knocking sent my already frayed nerves into a frenzy. The way my life was unfolding lately, it was probably someone about to deliver news of a tragic event that had happened or would happen soon.

My face remained aimed at the peephole even after I'd slammed my eyes shut. Dayton and Callie were out there, and they presented, bitch-open-this-door expressions I understood even through the narrow view. They would force me to spill my guts before they left this apartment tonight.

After running quick fingers through my hair, I slid my palms down my face. Nothing was taking the redness from my eyes or the puffiness from under them. They would notice I had been crying, and all hell would break loose.

After springing the door open, I stepped aside and gestured my hand for them to enter. Four concerned but demanding eyes landed on me and remained pinned there. Their necks swiveled as they stepped inside, their gazes staying locked on me. They made me feel like a child who'd finally been caught after hiding my misdeeds.

I stood facing the door after I locked it, preparing for the tongue lashing I was about to endure. When I turned and began to walk into my living room, my steps halted.

They were parked at the dining room table. They sat next to each other on the opposite side to make sure I sat in the hot seat.

"Ladies," I said as I approached the table. This was going to be bad. Callie's usual smile was a grimace while serious lines stretched across Dayton's forehead.

Before my butt brushed the seat, Dayton started.

"What in the whole entire fuck is going on, Charla? And don't give us bullshit about you and the *asshole* working shit out. I want to know the real deal."

My tears began to flow, changing their expressions from serious to concerned. My friends jumped out of their chairs and marched around the table to me.

Callie threw her arms around my shoulders and planted her cheek against mine. Dayton stood on the opposite side of me, holding my shaking hand.

"Charla, I wasn't trying to be an asshole. We just want to know what's going on because it's obvious something is wrong. You know we care about you and only want what's best for you. Shit, we just sat in my car for an hour, trying to figure out how to get that asshole to leave. Callie called that motherfucker, reporting that one of his employees had set one of their clients' buildings on fire," Dayton stated, tightening her grip on my hand.

A smile broke through the tight grips of dread at their antics. The lengths they would go through to check on me put together a few pieces of my broken heart. I squeezed them to me and released a long-winded sob. I loved these ladies with all I had and was damned lucky to have them in my life.

"Thank you for doing that for me," I choked out. "Carter," was all I could get out on my second attempt at speaking.

"That motherfucker didn't hit you, did he?" came Dayton's angry words.

Carter had never put his hands on me, but his threats had the same effect as if he did.

"No. He didn't hit me, but he may as well have."

"Do I need to go get my gun?" came Dayton's voice. "I'll call my daddy and brothers to do a gang beatdown on that bastard until he's pissing blood."

Her protective offer had me grinning through my tears. Although the idea of Carter getting gang-beaten was an appealing one, I would never let Dayton and Callie jeopardize the work they poured into building respectful lives. However, Dayton's suggestion reminded me that someone had already given Carter the beat down he deserved.

"No. You don't need to go and get your gun or order Carter the ass whipping he desperately needs."

My eyes were so puffy they were like two weights set into my eye sockets.

Dayton broke up our group huddle. She took my hand and dragged me to my couch, where she and Callie sat on either side of me. They angled their bodies to face me on each side. Callie reached under my small in-table and grabbed a Kleenex.

"What did that motherfucker do?" Dayton asked once we were all settled on the couch. "You know I never liked his pretty-boy punk ass. Asshole son-of-a-bitch."

I couldn't help a watery laugh at Dayton's disdain for Carter. Blowing my nose, I sniffed a few times before my words squeaked out.

"He recorded me and Ransome having sex. He threatened to show the recording to my bosses if I didn't take him back and stay away from Ransome. He even threatened to burn down Ransome's barbershop and house if I didn't comply."

Dayton's head jerked back. "You mean to tell me Mr. Stripper Man got property and a barbershop? Well, damn."

Callie cut her eyes at Dayton for the part of my comment she had chosen to focus on.

"You have to go to the police. Carter recorded you and Ransome without your permission, which means he is blackmailing you with illegal evidence and threatening someone's livelihood with arson."

I swallowed hard, shaking my head at the notion of what else hung over my head.

"That's not the worst of it. When I tried to leave anyway, he threatened to take the sex tape to his police buddies and tell them that Ransome broke in here and raped me. He said he'd fix the door to make it look like a break-in and that his police friends would make sure Ransome would not only go to prison but get dealt with while in there."

Dayton shook her head. "That motherfucking asshole!"

"He can't do that and get away with it," Callie added.

A deep sigh left Dayton.

"Callie, you know as well as I do. Carter may as well be the cops. He knows the ins and outs of the law, and he runs the largest security firm in this area. Going to the cops against him won't mean a damn thing. You have to fight a demon-face devil like him with fire," Dayton spat.

"How?" Callie asked.

A smile crept slowly across my lips as I eyed Dayton. She must have spotted the moment I acknowledged what she was suggesting.

"If I'm going to get myself away from Carter, save my career, and keep him from destroying Ransome, I'm going to have to get dirt on him. I'm going to have to be as devious as he's been with me. I'm going to have to do a lot of shit I don't like and not get caught while doing it. Thankfully, I've already begun digging up that dirt."

"You won't be doing it alone," Callie said. The conviction in her tone was genuine.

Dayton had a far-off stare on her face. "Hell no, she's not doing this shit alone."

I knew the look. Dayton was already thinking of all the ways she could torture Carter. When a twisted smile formed on her lips, I knew she meant business.

"Carter thinks he has you over a barrel. For now, he does, but he's about to find out how devious a woman can be when he backs her into a corner," Dayton said, like it was some sort of foregone prophecy.

Instead of breaking down and crying like I assumed I would, my spirits were lifted for the first time in weeks. I felt even better after I told Dayton and Callie about the investigator I hired and about Carter getting jumped last night.

Chapter Twenty-nine

Charla

A week later.

"He just left."

The text went out to Dayton the moment Carter drove off, and his taillights disappeared. Less than a minute later, forty-three seconds to be exact, Dayton's car came into view. She and Callie had already been parked inside the condo complex, waiting until I sent them a message that Carter had left.

Like clockwork, Carter left between six and eight p.m., and I was sure he wouldn't return until midnight or later. He was likely checking on his baby momma but choosing to live with me to keep his eyes on me. I knew Carter. He was biding his time until I changed my mind about us getting back together.

I flipped the locks and cracked the door open for Dayton and Callie. Dayton walked in like a detective, glancing around for what, I have no idea. Callie walked past her and slung her arms around my neck.

"You okay?"

"I'm good," I replied, giving her a tight squeeze. Dayton joined the hug, crashing her body into ours before we broke apart.

"Let me see the address for the apartment," Dayton requested, wiggling her fingers at me. "I want to see if it rings any bells."

Callie stared upside her head, her eyes asking questions before she voiced them.

"Why? You planning on going over there?" Callie asked, teasingly.

"Hell, yeah. We need to at least see if the asshole's car is going to be there," Dayton replied.

The statement made my brows shoot up to my hairline. I'd told them that the detective had discovered an apartment that Carter was leasing, but he didn't have any information yet on who Carter may or may not have been living there with. Me, Dayton, and Callie naturally assumed he was renting the place for his baby momma.

"I was being nosey, seeing if I could dig up some dirt on him. The investigator can tell me if he rented the place for someone else and even get us pictures," I added.

Dayton kept her hand out, her unblinking gaze pinned on mine. "Let me see the address, please."

I didn't even bother fussing with her. She was the boldest of us all and would go driving her crazy butt over there to be nosey.

"I'll make us some drinks," Callie called out while I went into the spare bedroom I was living in to retrieve the address. I was never one of those women who spied on her boyfriend, but Carter had turned me into an aspiring detective. Finding information to free myself from him was my new obsession despite hiring an investigator.

When I stepped back into the living room, Callie handed me a drink. I didn't even ask what it was before taking a sip and handing Dayton the piece of paper.

"Prosper Pines, 812 Battery Court Apartment 210," Dayton mumbled the information. "I know where this is. Cancel those drinks," she said, eyeballing the glasses of fruity-delight and joy-bringing beverages Callie had mixed for us.

I wasn't driving, so I wasn't ditching my drink. Neither did Callie. Besides, Dayton couldn't have been serious. Spying on Carter at the level of going over to his pregnant girlfriend's house made me look crazy. It meant that I would be doing some real stalker shit.

"Put your shoes on, and let's go," Dayton commanded. She was serious. The thought of being nosey enticed me, but I couldn't do this and let my friends tag along. Although, I wouldn't have minded getting a glimpse at who Carter had left me for and where she lived.

"I am not going over there and starting any mess. I don't even care that he has someone else. I just need dirt on him."

"Who said anything about starting a mess? If it's dirt you want, I'm willing to bet my next paycheck that it will be at that apartment. Besides, we are just going to go take a quick peek."

Me and Callie flashed Dayton sharp eyes.

"You're lying your ass off. You have been and always will be the one to get shit started," I stated while sliding my feet into a pair of tennis shoes and grabbing my wallet and keys.

***

Twenty minutes later.

I rode shotgun while Callie sat in the back, her body leaning through the opening to the front seat so we all had the same view.

We drove into the moderate-looking apartment complex situated in a decent neighborhood, surrounded by middle-class homes tucked a few miles away from what would be considered low-income and crime-ridden. Carter was financially able to do better than this for the woman who carried his child, but it wasn't my business.

The eight or nine buildings surrounding the three-story building with the pool and housing office were flanked by trees in the back, another apartment complex to the right, and a residential neighborhood to the left. The buildings had a brick facade at the bottom and white stucco on the second level.

The gate around the complex was a deterrent as the front was open to the public with signs warning against trespassing. Dayton drove us into the place like we lived there while my neck was on a constant swivel, searching for the apartment number.

"There's his SUV right there," Callie said, pointing out Carter's black BMW while we rolled slowly past the building that housed apartment 210 on the second floor. The apartments were relatively new, and you needed a key code to get into each building.

"What now," I asked?"

Callie shrugged.

"I don't know. I've never stalked anyone before," she said.

"It's not stalking. Carter asked for this smoke when he blackmailed me." My words were low but stern enough to cause Callie and Dayton to cast dim glances in my direction.

"Amen," Dayton added. "He was the one who declared war."

Dayton eased the car into a parking spot in a dark corner at the other end of the building. It was far enough away that if Carter left, he wouldn't see us but close enough to have a view of the apartment.

"Isn't that them?" Dayton asked, sitting up in her seat. She leaned closer to my side to see the couple walking toward the parking lot. We'd only been sitting there for five minutes. I knew Carter's walk and build a mile away, so the dim setting didn't do much to conceal his identity.

"That's him," I confirmed.

"I can't see the bitch's face, but she's skinny as hell for someone who's supposed to be pregnant."

"No need for name-calling," I reprimanded Dayton. "The poor woman probably has no idea she's being played."

Dayton didn't reply to my comment because it had likely gone in one ear and out the other.

Carter and his baby momma climbed into his SUV, and he didn't even bother to get the door for the woman carrying his child.

"What now?" Callie asked once they drove off.

"What the hell do you mean? *What now?*" Dayton asked the question like we already knew the answer. "We have been given an opportunity to get dirt on Carter's grimy ass. I say we go in there and find it."

"What?" I gasped the question, staring in Dayton's direction. "We can't just go waltzing in there. One, it's illegal. Two, we don't know how long they'll be gone, and three, do any of you know how to pick a lock?"

"Baby momma had a purse and a sweater slung across her arm. The only reason a woman would want an extra layer in the summertime is if they're going to some-place that might be a little chilly. I think they're going to a restaurant, movies, or something," Callie pointed out.

Her assessment had Dayton and me glancing back at her, impressed.

"What?" she asked with a sheepish grin. "I watch CSI and Law and Order."

"Okay, detectives, how do you propose we get in?" I asked, my gaze bouncing back and forth between them.

Was I sitting here considering my first breaking and entering? However, I couldn't let Carter ruin mine and Ransome's lives when he'd been the one doing dirt the entire time.

"Easy," Dayton pointed, and me and Callie's eyes followed where her finger was aimed—at the apartment right in front of us.

"If you climb the neighbor's patio fence, it will get you high enough to reach the second-floor balcony. No one locks their patio door, so I'd bet the same paycheck I wagered earlier that's the way in."

Callie leaned closer and squinted at the alignment of the patios. The person on the first floor had thick white wood fences around their little patio area for privacy. The thick fences were tall enough that they would provide a good boost up to the next level.

"I think it's doable," Callie finally agreed. I was scared but open to anything to get back at Carter. The alcohol in my system must have been doing its job because I finally agreed that the stunt could be done.

"Who's coming in with me?" I asked.

"Me."

"Me."

"You both can't go in. We need a lookout. Someone has to blow the horn to get our attention if they get back before we get out of there."

Callie leaned across the console to get a good look at my face, and Dayton gave me a proud side-eye.

"You sure you haven't done this shit before," Dayton asked playfully.

"I don't watch Law and Order, but I read the hell out of crime and suspense dramas."

"I'll stay in the car," Callie volunteered.

Dayton cranked her car.

"What are you doing?" I questioned, hoping they didn't hear the apprehension in my tone at the prospect of doing something so dangerous and illegal.

"I'm parking closer so we can hear the horn, and Callie can have the car running and waiting for us in case we have to move fast."

After parking, we sat in silence. The night was alive, only broken apart by moonlight and the light on the tall metal poles throughout the complex.

Dayton opened her door, and I jumped. My heart hammered in my chest, but I found the will to grip the handle of the door and plant my feet on the ground.

Dayton peeked back into the car. "Callie, come with us for now in case we need a little boost."

Callie didn't reply but simply swung the back door open and stepped out. We followed Dayton, the boldest and most fiercest of us. Like the detectives we'd become, she peered over the fence to check the status of the first-floor occupants.

"They're up, but no one's in the living room. This shit is higher than it appeared from inside the car. Give me a boost, Charla," Dayton said, still inspecting the balcony alignment.

Dayton placed her hands on the top of the thick wood and heaved herself up, and I wedged my shoulder under her left ass cheek and boosted her higher."

We hadn't planned this out too well. How the hell was she supposed to stand atop the fence and reach up to the floor of the balcony above? Dayton's feet slipped along the white wood, but she heaved, and I shoved until her top half went over and her legs were in the air.

I placed a hand over my heart and one over my mouth to stifle a gasp, thinking she would fall, but she didn't.

"Oh. Thank God," I whispered.

Callie was on her job, scanning to see if we'd attracted any attention. Dayton positioned her body to straddle the fence, balancing herself on one ass cheek while lifting her foot to place it to allow her to stand. I wasn't sure I had that kind of dexterity, but I'd soon find out.

On one leg, Dayton meticulously balanced herself until she stood fully upright and could place her wobbly feet firmly on the top of the fence.

She reached above herself and was just able to grip the bar of the metal railing that enclosed the balcony above. This part of her journey would involve a test of her strength.

It was my turn now. I reached up and gripped the top of the fence. Although the top of it was narrow, the surface was flat and provided a stable enough foundation that helped me understand how Dayton was able to stand on it. I dragged myself up, grunting as my shoes slid along the side, fighting for traction.

With me bent across the fence and leaning into someone's personal property, I heaved and willed my legs up enough for the heel of my right foot to catch at the top of the fence. A few grunts and not-so-flattering wiggling, I finally bent my body until I resembled a pretzel and could straddle the fence.

The hard wood pressing into my ass crack had me wincing with every move, but I had to endure it to keep my balance. Whatever buzz I had from the alcohol was long gone.

I focused on staying on this fence and not falling and busting my ass on the wrong side of illegal. My right leg shook under my weight as one foot remained lifted for balance, along with my outstretched arms. No man was worth this kind of indignity.

I reached up and damn near fell my ass down when something caught a hold of my forearm and ankle. It was Dayton from above me and Callie below me.

"The doors are open," Dayton whispered the update while tugging my arm. "I'll pull this arm, and you use your other to lift until you can get your legs up."

Sweating and grunting like I was constipated, I didn't want to think about what I must look like scaling a fence and scrambling to reach the balcony of the apartment above it. It took three heart-pounding tries with Dayton's help to get one of my legs up on the balcony for the extra leverage I needed to climb up and over the metal railing.

When my feet landed flat on the other side, my legs wobbled, but Dayton hadn't released her grip on my arms, which helped keep me on my feet. I could do nothing but stand there with a hand atop my heart and breathe.

Dayton waved into the night, and I turned in time to see Callie return a wave before she headed back to the car. Breathing like I'd run a marathon, I followed Dayton, who left the sliding door into the apartment open for me to enter.

The new-house smell permeated the air. The sparsely furnished place had boxes that Carter's sidepiece hadn't fully unpacked yet.

A couch, loveseat, end table, and fifty-inch television mounted to the wall were all that made up the living room.

The tall standing lamp sitting next to the couch had been left on.

"Dayton," I whisper-yelled after her when she took off toward the bedroom. I was so damn nervous that my hands shook while I conjured up images of all the different ways SWAT would knock the door down and open fire on us.

Was I really standing in my ex-boyfriend's pregnant girlfriend's apartment?

"Charla, come here," Dayton called out, making me jump. "I think I've hit the jackpot."

Glancing back at the open balcony door, I headed in her direction. To say that I was terrified was an understatement.

You have to do this. He's blackmailing you and Ransome, I reminded myself.

A queen-sized bed was covered with a cheap pink cotton comforter slung haphazardly over the top. The bed sat against the wall furthest from the window. A dresser that matched the shiny, cheaply-made headboard of the bed sat at the foot. Like in the living room, unpacked boxes sat untouched.

Dayton was rummaging through one. I didn't waste time arguing with my moral compass. I opened the box nearest me and began rifling through it. It was filled with clothing that appeared to have all come from Forever 21.

I left the box alone and went to the dresser. On the top of it were several books and student identification badges. Had Carter gone back to college to shop for another unsuspecting younger woman he could control and cheat on? My eyes must have been mistaken.

"Dayton," I called out, but my voice was so low that I had to call out again for her to hear me while she swept through what must have been the third box she'd opened.

"Dayton, come check this out?"

"What? You found something?" she returned.

My head nodded absently, my eyes riveted to the words on the identification badge. Dayton stepped up, more concerned about my stunned expression than what was causing it.

"Look," I urged, pointing at the badge.

She leaned down and read the words out loud.

"Nicola Haywood. Roosevelt Morris High School." Dayton paused and stared at the badge for a few seconds, processing the implications the words written on it conveyed.

"What the fuck? You mean to tell me that demon has gotten a high schooler pregnant. This child better not be underage, or his ass is going to jail."

"Maybe this is his new lady's daughter," I said. Hoping the poor girl wasn't being taken advantage of.

"There is only one way to find out. We keep searching," Dayton suggested.

And we kept searching until Dayton came running out of the closet holding up a stack of papers and a purse.

"Carter's blackmailing ass is going to jail," she said with a breathless tone and a huge smile on her face. I held up the lease paperwork I found.

We sat our findings on the bed, and Dayton and I withdrew our phones. I pointed at the names on the lease that listed Carter as the owner of the apartment and Nicola Haywood as an occupant, confirming that the girl was his girlfriend.

Dayton and I snapped several photos before her finger tap danced against a badly-copied birth certificate.

"Found this and her social security card in one of her old purses. This child is seventeen. She has her eighteenth birthday coming up in two months, but that doesn't excuse the fact that she's underage and pregnant."

Dayton yanked more paperwork from the old purse. It included the sonogram of the baby and other medical paperwork. There was even a stack of photos of the girl. One caught my attention.

"That must be her parents," I said, my brain working overtime to figure out why the man in the picture, with his arm wrapped protectively around the girl and his wife, looked familiar.

"Where the hell do I know this man from?" I questioned, snapping a photo.

Dayton was giving the photo the same quizzical eye as me. She snapped her fingers, trying to make the recognition come to life in her brain.

"Damn!" she said.

"What?" I asked, desperate to know what she'd come up with.

"You and everyone in the city knows that man because he's on every other billboard and city bus in this damn city. That's Nicholas Haywood, one of the most high-powered attorneys in this city, maybe even in this state."

My hand flew up to my mouth.

"And Carter has knocked up his underaged daughter."

Dayton continued to shake her head. "I'm willing to bet her parents don't know, or Carter would be in jail right now."

"I feel sorry for that young girl. She's probably think-ing, like I did, that she has the best man in the world."

I shook my head, disgusted by Carter's behavior but not surprised after what he was currently doing to me.

"Let's get out of here before they come back. This should be enough that even his cop friends would frown on him."

We straightened the things we rifled through, climbed down the balcony, which was easier going down than coming up, and walked back to Dayton's car that Callie had running and ready to roll if things went sideways.

Dayton jumped into the passenger side while I climbed into the back. Callie drove us back to her place instead of mine since it was the closest. We exited the car in silence, processing all that we had discovered.

The adventure we'd just experienced paled in com-parison to what Carter was doing.

After Callie fixed us drinks, she and Dayton sat sip-ping and staring at me.

"I will meet with the investigator in a few more days. I'm going to wait and see what else he found before I con-front Carter," I informed them, knowing what was on their minds.

Chapter Thirty

Charla

A week and many arguments later, Carter walked into the spare bedroom I continued to occupy. He stared with that determined and demanding expression he'd begun to cast in my direction lately. I turned my lip up at him and kept packing.

"What are you doing, Charla?"

"What's it look like I'm doing? I'm packing my shit to get the hell away from your crazy ass."

"So, you don't care about me messing up your career or your little boyfriend's life?"

I gave a light pat to the shirt I laid on top of the stack of shirts I was about to place inside my suitcase. Staring down at the clothing for a long moment, I took a deep breath to calm my nerves before I glanced up at Carter.

He crept closer to the bed, glancing back and forth between me and my packed suitcase. I'm sure the deranged gleam in my eyes helped put that hint of reluctance in his gaze. I eyeballed him for at least a straight minute before I said anything.

"If you touch my life or Ransome's, I guarantee you that your life is going to get messed up right along with ours. You're not the only one who can blackmail someone."

His face scrunched in confusion, and his posture stiffened. He was probably waiting for me to elaborate, but I wanted him to know how it felt to have shit hanging over his head. I turned back to the suitcase and continued to pack.

"You aren't leaving this condo, Charla." That smug ass expression of his had returned. "You know I *can*, and I *will* make good on my promises."

I smiled but didn't glance up.

"I know you can. You've been fucking people over since I met you. That's why after all these years, I've pulled my head out of my ass and wised up. I found some dirt on you. Well, in your case, it's not dirt, the shit is mud."

I walked off and entered the closet, leaving him staring after me. I exited the closet, dragging my second suitcase that was already packed. He still hadn't said anything but stood there like his presence alone would intimidate me.

I proceeded to the bathroom for my toiletries. When I returned, Carter was in the same place, his body weighted with tension. There was no doubt in my mind that he was trying to piece together in his head the dirt I'd dug up on him. As soon as he fixed his mouth to utter a word, the doorbell rang.

"Excuse me," I said as I marched past him to answer the door.

Callie was right on time. She was happy to let me stay in her guest bedroom until I found a place of my own. Carter's stiff gaze lingered on her, following me into the bedroom.

"Hey, Carter, how's it going?" Callie said with a smirk on her face.

He flashed a quick eye roll and didn't bother to greet her in return.

It was no secret Carter didn't like my friends. He claimed they were too nosey and involved in my life. Through the years, they had no problems confronting and calling him on his bullshit. I was the one who usually played peacemaker.

"I don't know where the hell you think you're going, but you're not leaving this house," he continued his demand. He and Callie trailed me as I strolled back toward the bedroom.

He stepped in and grabbed my arm when I reached for my suitcase. Callie stepped in front of me. I jerked my arm away from him and eased her out of the way. I didn't know what Carter was capable of, and the last thing I needed was him putting his hands on my friend.

"Keep your hands off of me. How dare you grab me like that, you rapist!"

My words had him backing up and shaking his head.

"You know good and damn well I didn't rape you, Charla."

"I'm not talking about me."

Callie's head shifted back and forth between us. She and Dayton had demanded to be here with me when I confronted Carter. Thankfully, Dayton had an appointment she couldn't miss.

"I'm talking about your underaged baby momma."

His eyes widened, and his mouth hung so wide open it appeared he was attempting to unhinge his jaw.

"That's right. I know your dirty little secret. You got that child pregnant, and you're giving her whatever she wants to keep her quiet."

"You're talking out of your ass, Charla. You can't prove or back up any of the shit you're accusing me of."

A condescending smile crept across my lips. Callie took a few steps back and sat on my bed as Carter and I continued to stand on either side of her.

"I have a copy of her birth certificate. She won't be an adult until after she's had that baby. I know that her parents kicked her out after you got her pregnant. I'm guessing because she refused to tell them who the father was. I even know that you have her living in Prosper Pines, apartment number 210."

He was frozen—only his blinking eyes indicated that he was still breathing.

"You have a minor living in an apartment you're leasing in your name. An underaged pregnant girl, Carter? Umh. Umh. Umh. You sure know how to pick them. The best part is she's the underaged daughter of a prominent, well-respected lawyer."

Carter blinked. He couldn't have spit out a single word if I'd put my hand up his ass and turned him into my puppet. This was the first time I saw his arrogant ass speechless. In my peripheral vision, I spotted the proud smile on Callie's face.

Carter turned to Callie and pointed at the bedroom door.

"Get out! Me and Charla need to discuss our personal affairs in private."

Callie blasted him with a mean scowl.

"You must be out of your rabid-ass mind if you think I'm leaving my friend in here with a damned rapist."

Callie's comment surprised the hell out of me and made Carter sputter. Dayton would have been proud. Besides, this was no longer just about me. An innocent young girl who was being manipulated was now in the equation.

After Callie's comment, she glanced in my direction like she was telling me to keep spilling more of Carter's beans. Who was I to hold up the progress of this discussion, so I continued.

"Oh, and your girlfriend, City Councilman Lawrence Wells', wife. She's pregnant, too. "

Again, his mouth dropped open and remained in the position. Carter couldn't get me pregnant, so he'd gone out and made two babies. It hurt that he'd done this to me, but it was also the wake-up call that I desperately needed. His actions lifted the blinders I'd been wearing for years.

I enjoyed seeing him wear shock like it was his new face. I noticed the moment when the expression changed to one of anger.

"She's not my girlfriend, and what does her pregnancy have to do with me?" He attempted to defend himself while sending subtle glances in Callie's direction.

"Carter. For such a smart man, you're dumb as hell. For someone who works in the security field, I assumed you'd have at least done homework on the woman you cheated on me with."

At this point, Callie had leaned back a bit on the bed, enjoying the show.

"Maxine Wells is three months pregnant, and soon, she's not going to be able to hide that belly from her husband. A husband who had a vasectomy a few years ago."

I spotted Callie from the corner of my eye, covering her mouth with her hands. The tea I was spilling now had come from the detective a few hours ago, so I'd not had a chance to tell her and Dayton.

Sweat glistened at Carter's hairline and top lip. I don't believe he'd known that his other girlfriend was pregnant too. He couldn't say anything in defense of himself after I released that bit of information. I slung my purse across my shoulder before turning and gripping the handle of my suitcase.

Callie stood at this point and grabbed my second suitcase without me having to tell her to do so.

I strolled past Carter, making sure the wheels of my suitcase ran over his foot. He yelped and hopped back as his eyes shot holes in the back of my head. I stopped and allowed Callie to pass by me as I turned back to Carter.

"If I were an evil woman, I would file charges against you for filming me without my permission. I suggest you get rid of everything you have on me and forget every notion you have of messing up my life and Ransome's. If not, I'll leak your secrets to the press so fast, your fucking head is going to spin clean off your damn body."

I left him with those words. There wasn't much he could do in the way of damage control because Callie was a witness to our conversation. Also, Douglas Roberts, my private investigator, had managed to wipe the videos Carter had of me and Ransome from his phone and computer. I would never know if Carter had any other copies out there, but if he was as scared as his bewildering expression suggested about his secrets getting out, he would do the right thing.

Also, I couldn't sit by and allow him to abuse the underaged girl he'd impregnated, so Mr. Roberts had come up with a covert way to get him caught with that child without it coming back on me. I don't believe his police friends had enough power to keep him out of jail once that girl's powerful attorney of a father found out who his underaged daughter was pregnant by. Carter was going to be in for one hell of a fight.

Chapter Thirty-one

Charla

Two weeks of self-reflection had done me good. I hadn't heard one word from Carter, which was good news as far as I was concerned. I took some of Callie's advice and chilled for as long as I needed to. I didn't go chasing after Ransome right away because I needed to get over Carter's betrayal and think about what I truly wanted from the man that would be in my life.

Before I turned the knob and shoved the door to the shop open, I took a big chest-rising breath. A bell chimed as my heels clicked against the shiny, gray and white marble floor. I took in the modernized décor before inquisitive eyes zoomed in my direction from every corner of the open space. The sound of multiple conversations began lowering with every step I took.

A pair of caramel-colored platform heels hugged my feet. A baby blue wrap dress clung to my curves in all the right places and revealed a smidgen of cleavage. My hair had been freshly washed, straightened, and styled with a line of side braids that added an edgy vibe to my sleek look.

I made sure I smelled as fresh as a breeze whispering through a field of sunflowers. My clutch, which matched my shoes, hung loosely in my hand. If I was going to go groveling back to Ransome, I wanted to look good doing it.

It was difficult to ignore the eyes on me, but I searched for the green set that mattered. Clippers stopped buzzing, scissors stopped shearing away hair, razors stopped edging necks, and individuals sitting in red leather barber's chairs craned their necks to see what had caused this male-dominated domain to go so quiet.

Flashes of lust, interest, and what I believed was approval sparked behind the gazes locked on me. Even the kid sweeping the floor stood in place with the broom in his hand and his gaze raking over me.

When I spotted Ransome, our gazes locked. He stood above a man, holding a set of clippers in one hand and a small-toothed black comb in the other. Like everyone else, he stood frozen with his gaze fixed on me. I think the man's hair he worked on was one of his friends and a dancer from the club.

Hesitantly, I took a few steps closer, fighting to keep my nervousness at bay. I was afraid he wouldn't want to have anything else to do with me after I dumped him for Carter, let him fuck me in a public bathroom, and then dumped him all over again.

Privacy was not a luxury in this place, so I walked to within a foot of Ransome. My five-inch heels put my eyes a few inches below his. I kept my voice low. "Is there a place we can talk?"

The tightness around his eyes didn't ease the anxiousness riding me. He pointed toward the back of the shop but remained silent after he sat the comb and clippers on the counter behind him.

When we began to walk away, the man whose hair he was cutting, sat up and stared after us.

"Ran, are you seriously going to leave me halfway through a cut?" the man called after Ransome.

Another man said, "If a lady that looks like that walked in here wanting to talk to me, I'd leave your narrow ass in hell."

The group laughed, and a little of their conversations picked up, but I sensed eyes on us. I followed Ransome to the back of the shop. To the left of us was an open stock area with boxes of goods stacked neatly on large floor-to-ceiling metal shelves. Across from the stock area was a door with a large restroom sign attached.

Ransome stopped at the last door, extending into a narrow hallway. He used his keys to gain access to the room, stood in the doorway, and pointed me inside.

It was his office, nice and professionally furnished. The sight impressed me like the rest of the place. A large black leather chair sat behind a huge, highly varnished, redwood desk. Two golden, cashmere-covered chairs sat in front of it. The remaining empty wall was lined with three sets of four-drawer file cabinets.

The picture that hung on the wall behind his desk wasn't of dogs shooting pool—it was three perfectly aligned frames of vintage black and whites of barber's equipment. Either Ransome had designing skills, or he'd had his office professionally done.

This was not what I expected to see in a barbershop office, but it spoke volumes about the way Ransome carried and presented himself. I'd even been curious enough to stalk his social media accounts where he posted about his business and had racked up over a hundred thousand followers.

I inched my way to one of the chairs in front of his desk. He chose to post up right in front of me, leaning his tall, sexy body against the desk. He was dressed stylishly in a baby blue polo shirt, relaxed jeans, and expensive slip-ons.

My nervousness shifted up a gear from the stern gaze he had locked on me. Prolonging this discussion was useless, so my words began to spill out.

"I left Carter. He was blackmailing me to stay with him. I'd rather not say what he was blackmailing me with, but it was bad enough to make me stay when it was the last thing in the world I wanted."

His gaze and posture transformed, and before I knew it, Ransome knelt before me, his hands at my waist.

"Are you okay? Did he hurt you? What do you need me to do? Is he still blackmailing you? Is he going to retaliate now that you've left him?"

His reaction brightened my mood instantly. I placed my hand atop his arms to stop his questions. This was the kind of man I needed in my life. I'd hurt him, yet he jumped at the chance to see what I needed.

"It's all taken care of. I had to find a way to handle him on my own. I couldn't drag you into my mess. I'm staying with Callie until I find a place of my own. Carter and I are about as over as a couple can get."

"You can stay with me if you need a place to stay," he offered, the sincerity in his eyes shining through and melting my heart.

"I appreciate the offer, but no, thank you. I'm not going down that road with any man again. I can't make the same mistakes I made with Carter."

My grip on his muscular arm grew tighter.

"That being said, I'm not going to let Carter's behavior ruin any future relationships I might have. Which brings me to why I showed up at your barbershop unannounced."

I dropped my head and swallowed the lump that had formed in my throat. "I'm sorry I hurt you, Ransome. If I had any other choice in the way I had to deal with Carter…"

My throat grew so tight, it stuttered my words. Tears began to form, and my bottom lip trembled. Hurting Ransome had been one of the worst parts of this whole ordeal.

He leaned in closer. His worried expression further proved that he was a different caliber of man than Carter. Here I was, the one who had hurt him, and he was worried about me.

I placed a caring palm against his cheek, and he leaned into it. Those big, pretty eyes of his radiated so much care, I would have been a straight fool not to believe that we had something special.

"I don't know what we are, you and I, but I would like to explore it further if you—"

He lifted higher on his knees. "Yes. Of course. I would like nothing more," he said, not letting me get the complete sentence out.

When his lips went crashing into mine, I kissed him and laughed against his anxious mouth at the same time. After a thorough kiss, I placed my hands on either side of his face.

"I was worried that you wouldn't want me back after the way I walked away from you."

His eyes searched mine, and the emotion shining in his gaze tore into me, splitting my heart wide open.

"Nothing else matters. I'll always want you, Charlene. I love you."

"I love you, too," I said, my words sure this time.

His gaze froze on mine after I said those words. I believed I'd shocked him as much as I surprised myself. I flashed him a wide smile.

"And I'm not talking myself out of the way I feel this time. I love you," I said once again before I placed a sweet kiss on his sexy lips. His smile widened against my mouth, causing me to giggle.

We laughed our way through the kiss. Happiness wasn't a strong enough word to describe how Ransome made me feel.

He stood and pulled me to my feet and against his strong body. "Why don't we go and grab lunch?"

"I would love that, but first..." I went up on my toes and placed another hot kiss on his lips before sucking his bottom lip between mine. It was the sweet part of the kiss before I sank my teeth into his lip and ran my tongue roughly across where I'd bitten. The action drew a groan from Ransome, and it was all that was needed to get his blood flowing.

He reached around my waist and drew me more securely into him. The bulge that was starting to grow in his pants pressed against my stomach as his strong hand palmed the globes of my ass. Our heavy breathing filled the space of his office.

"Ransome," I whispered hotly against his lips.

"Yes," he hissed out against my mouth.

"I need you to fuck me right now."

"It will be my pleasure," he replied while reaching down to pick up the hem of my dress. I assisted him by tugging the tie on the dress and opening the front with one sweep of my hand.

His hands flowed along the contours of my body and glided along the hot flesh of my hips.

Ransome spun us so my back was to his desk. He walked me back until we bumped into it. He reached around me and swiped whatever was on top of his desk onto the floor. Items crashed, but I was too busy undoing his pants and yanking at his shirt to see what was falling.

As soon as he cleared a space on his desk, he swept my dress up like it was a cape, lifted and sat me on the shiny hardwood finish. He reached down with one hand, gripped the tail of his shirt at his stomach, and lifted. I assisted in getting it over his head since I'd failed at getting it off of him earlier.

The need that had taken us by storm was so urgent that we didn't bother wasting any more time. He grabbed the front of my underwear and snatched them so hard, they came off like paper. He took a deep, eye-closing sniff of them before tossing them across his shoulder.

As soon as he stood and bent to give me another steamy kiss, I hooked my fingers in the waistband of his jeans and boxers. Without taking his mouth away from mine, he assisted by shoving his pants midway down his legs. As soon as his thick and heavy dick popped out, he slid me closer to the edge of the desk, aligning me with what he was about to fill me with.

He stared into my eyes as if asking permission, and I spread my legs in reply to his silent plea. I used one of my hands to hold his bobbing dick steady, and the other had a grip around his toned ass to pull him in.

The first magnificent thrust he gave caused me to gasp and dig my nails into his tight ass cheek. He stilled with a frozen stare as our bodies reunited.

When he backed half out and plunged back into me, the force of his sensational stroke closed my eyes. He repeated the rhythm that had me begging for him not to stop. I could vaguely hear the grunt of the desk scraping across the floor with each thrust he delivered.

"Oh. Shit. So good," he roared.

I was a mess of hissing sighs and high-pitched moans. When I could form words, the loud, "You're fucking me so good," phrases echoed throughout his office. The space became a funnel for our explicit need to voice our experiences.

"You're making my pussy yours," was yelled out repeatedly as I glanced down, awed at the sight of his dick pumping in and out of me. "God, it's all yours."

Since the desk wasn't nailed to the floor, it continued to grunt loudly, protesting our aggressive usage. Ransome lifted me, keeping our connection while walking us away from his desk. I had no idea what we knocked over, but something went crashing to the floor. The next thing I knew, I had a wall against my back with Ransome pinned in between my splayed legs.

I draped my arms tightly around his neck. Once he was satisfied with our new positioning, he began pounding into me. The sound of his body slamming into mine competed with my back and ass bumping against the wall.

We were lost in the sensations we drew from each other. The intoxication of this scene had me so far gone that I said shit that I probably would have given second thought to had I been in my right mind.

"Tell me again that this is my pussy," Ransome whispered against my lobe before his lips tickled my skin. He licked down my neck until his hot tongue massaged the spot that got me revved up more than I already was.

"It's yours, baby. This pussy is all for you," I yelled, and he pumped into me even harder.

"Anytime you want it. It's yours. Oh, Ransome," I dragged out his name in that crying voice.

When I threatened to burst from the buildup from all the pleasure he pumped into me, I was rewarded with an explosive orgasm that dominated my state of mind. A choked series of, "Oh Gods," left my mouth.

Ransome followed with roars so loud I swore they added a depth of pleasure to my already shaking body.

If Ransome was experiencing anything close to what I felt, it was a miracle we didn't fall to the floor. This session had me so satisfied and relaxed that I could have fallen asleep right there pinned against the wall with Ransome's dick still buried inside me. His harsh breathing was like a small, warm wind tunnel against my ear and neck.

When he managed to ease his way out of me, he shuddered. The action caused a lazy, "Oh," to escape me. Once he let me down, I stood on the two limp noodles that had replaced my legs. I wobbled in my heels that had somehow remained clinging to my feet. Ransome kept a firm hand around my arm and waist, steadying me before assisting me to his desk.

I leaned against the desk with one hand pressed flat on the top, heaving for breaths. Ransome reached into one of his desk drawers and retrieved a small packet of baby wipes. He took his time wiping me clean.

Once my vision was restored, I noticed that he was completely naked. His pants and boxers had been lost in the process of our episode. Looking at him was starting to get me hot again, proof that I was insatiable when it came to this man. He was sweet enough to help me back into my dress before he redressed himself.

We had made a complete mess of his office. Most of the contents from the top of his desk had been thrown about the floor. We had knocked over the small table and lamp near his door. I couldn't even recall us walking that far away from his desk. If all of that wasn't bad enough,

Ransome's employees and customers could have heard us.

As loud and expressive as we were, the damned entire block likely heard us. My cheeks warmed, and Ransome must have understood why I was suddenly embarrassed.

"You think they heard us?"

He shrugged. "I don't know. I never imagined I'd be having sex in my office."

We took five more minutes putting ourselves back together as best we could. Ransome's handsome face was three shades of pink and flushed. His shirt was nowhere close to as crisp as it was when he'd stepped into his office. The red scratch marks on his neck couldn't be hidden.

My dress was passable enough for me to wear out in public and thankfully, I hadn't gotten it stained with the large amounts of juice Ransome had made flow from me.

His firm hand pressed into the small of my back.

"Are you ready?"

I nodded and stepped forward. Although my head was heavier, I lifted it a little higher than normal, motivating myself to be brave enough to walk past all these people who likely heard us fucking the shit out of each other.

He opened the door, but before I stepped into the hall, the question of his age popped into my brain.

"Ransome?"

"Yes."

"How old are you?"

His smile grew wide, and he paused a long time before he answered.

"I'll be twenty-four in about five months."

"Oh my God," I said, not meaning to say it out loud.

"What? Are you okay?" he questioned with a hint of mischief in his smile. He knew damn well I would be shocked by his age. It's why he hadn't revealed it until now. I uprooted my heavy legs and stepped out the door. I was in love with a man who wasn't even in his mid-twenties. I took a deep breath and released it with ease.

I was being silly. Wasn't I? Of course, I was being silly. Carter was twelve years older than Ransome. However, Ransome was twice as mature.

"I'm fine," I finally answered him before stepping forward. Ransome made me happy. He took care of me sexually, took interest in my physical desires, and showed concern about my emotional needs.

His hand remained on my back when he shoved the doors open and waited until I stepped into the hallway. My nerves grew more tense when we walked out of his office and exited the hallway to walk past the storage and restroom area.

When we opened the door and stepped onto the shop floor, the silence in the room confirmed my suspicions. Every person in the building had heard us and probably thought we were the biggest freaks in the city.

Inquisitive smiles greeted us as we stepped closer to the exit. Amused, embarrassed, and expressions of all kinds were aimed in our direction.

"So, Ransome, should I lock up?" The guy whose hair he hadn't finished asked. Someone else must have finished his haircut. I put my gaze on the exit as Ransome stopped to answer the man. "Yes. Appreciate it, man."

"No problem at all. You need me to clean up your office before I lock up? It sounded like furniture got moved around, things were knocked over, and there may even be structural damage," the man continued teasingly.

A loud series of laughs erupted and livened up the place. Their laughter enticed my smile even while my cheeks burned with embarrassment. I don't know how the hell Ransome kept a straight face.

"No need to do that, *Trent*. I'll take care of it later." The way he stressed Trent's name let me know that Ransome was giving him a warning.

We began to move again, but another voice stopped us before we could escape.

"Ransome, most of this damn barbershop wants to be you when we grow up. From what we heard, you're a God."

Unable to help it any longer, I burst into laughter after placing a hand over my embarrassed face. If a little teasing was all I had to endure to get Ransome back, then I was the lucky one. My laughter made Ransome's sexy lips turn up into a wide grin before he took my hand and led me out of his shop.

Ransome was love, *my* love. He didn't lie when he said he loved me. I believed it the first time he'd said it. I believed it when he looked at me. I believed it even when we weren't together. I never had that type of bond with Carter because his love had always been a lie. Now, I was free to explore the many other blessings love offered.

Epilogue

Seven and a half months later.

"Hold my hand now!" Charla growled as if possessed by the demon from *The Exorcist*. It felt like she'd already cracked two bones in my left hand, and now I had no choice but to hand her my right. Charla had likely gotten pregnant the day we got together in that hotel bathroom.

Since she'd never been able to carry a baby to term previously, we ignored all the signs, and she didn't go to the doctor until she was four months pregnant. For Charla, it was the longest she'd been able to carry.

We considered the pregnancy a blessing and prayed every day for our son to arrive healthy. Now, here we are, three and a half months later, and he'd refused to stay put for the remaining month and a half.

"Push baby, push," I cheered Charla on, along with the doctor and nurse. Although prominent stress lines stretched across her face, her beauty prevailed, and she even released a few smiles during the times the demon she'd swallowed disappeared.

"The baby's head emerged, and Charla's glossy-eyed, sweat-drenched, heaving body made her appear ready to pass out. After this, I would cater to her every need and whim. The pain, the emotional effects, the changes to her body. She was enduring a lot of drastic changes to bring our son into this world, and I vowed to remind myself of it often.

When she went into labor yesterday, she and I feared the worst, but I dared not show it. I convinced her that we wanted to see our son so badly, that he'd answered our prayers and decided to arrive early.

"Once more, baby. You're doing good," I urged. All of the sensation in my hand was gone, but I didn't care. I was witnessing a miracle that scared my soul from my body and, at the same time, gave me a joyful high that would last me a lifetime.

His little pale and wrinkled body looked like it fell into the doctor's hands. All of the sound was sucked from the room, and I couldn't exhale, or speak, or move. My eyes were glued to the little glob the doctor and nurse worked on. I couldn't see what they were doing and was too afraid to move to get a better view.

My gaze went to Charla, whose eyes were aimed in the direction of our son. The terror in her gaze ripped my heart from my chest.

"God, please. Please let this little guy…"

The loud wail stopped my prayer and filled the room with an overwhelming amount of relief. Joy followed along with emotions that hit me so hard that tears I didn't know were there spilled down my cheeks.

The night I told Charla she hadn't found the right father to have a child with, I secretly prayed that it could be me, never truly accepting that it was possible.

When I was a young kid, homeless and living on the streets, I believed my prayers were ignored. Little did I know, they were being heard the entire time. I just needed to be patient enough to see what was in store for me.

Ransome Calday Pearce Jr. was presented to us, his watery-eyed parents. He cried, kicked, and wiggled within his swaddling like a little wrinkled worm attempting to uproot itself from the ground.

I leaned in and placed a kiss on Charla's sweaty forehead before placing another on our son's. Miracles did happen. I had the one thing that I'd never had before, that I didn't think was in the cards for me. The priceless view before me surpassed my dreams—the magnificent portrait of *my* family.

End of Love Lied

Blind Date with a Book

Don't feel like shopping around for your next read? Grab yourself a Blind Date with a Book.

All you have to do is head on over to (https://www.michelewesley.com/category/all-products) pick a genre and leave the rest to me, Author Keta Kendric.

If this is your first time reading my books, Blind Date with a Book, is a fun way of introducing yourself to more of my books. If you've already read my books, I appreciate you, and offer blind book dates by other bestselling authors.

Birthday, holiday, or just-because, Blind Dates with a Book are great gift ideas for yourself, your book friends, or loved ones. These hot Blind Dates arrive in the mail autographed and beautifully wrapped with swag.

Head on over to my Website Shop where you can use the coupon code HOTDATE15 to get 15% off on your order.

Note: Also offering regular autographed paperback books if a blind date is not your cup of tea.

Author's Note

Readers, my sincere thank you for reading Love Lied. Please leave a review or star rating letting me and others know what you thought of the book. If you enjoyed it please check out the next books in the series. If you enjoyed any of my other books, please pass them along to friends or anyone you think would enjoy them.

Other Titles by Keta Kendric

The Twisted Minds Series:

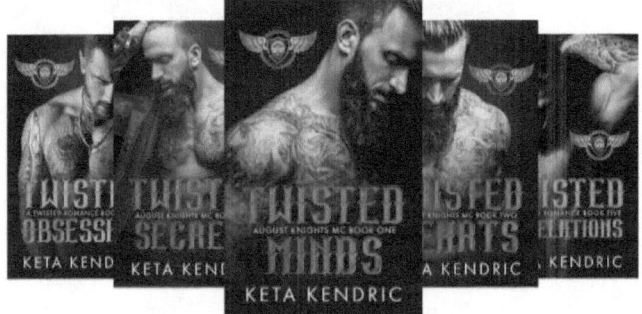

Twisted Minds #1
Twisted Hearts #2
Twisted Secrets #3
Twisted Obsession #4
Twisted Revelation #5
Twisted Deception # 6 (2024)

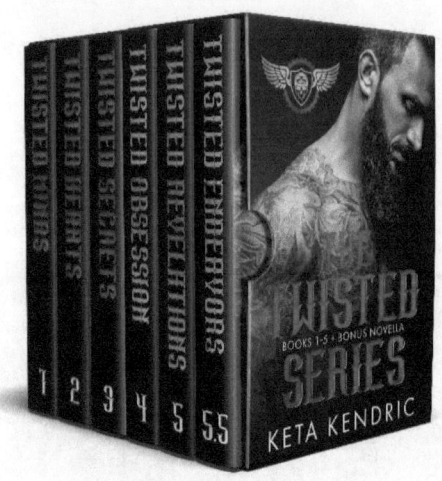

The Twisted Box Set

The Chaos Series:

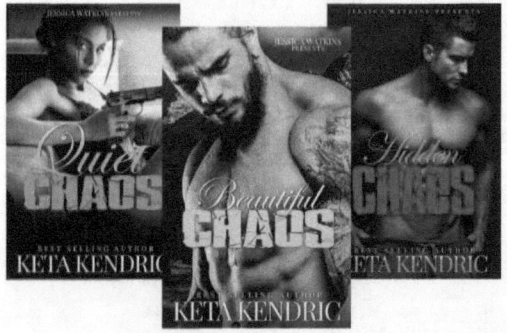

Beautiful Chaos #1
Quiet Chaos #2
Hidden Chaos#3

The Love Series

Love Lied #1
Love Whispered #2
Love Lingered #3

Stand Alones:

Severe

Roots of the Wicked

Primo DeLuca

Brizio DeLuca

Novellas:

Carolina Reaper

Mystery Meat

Spice Cake

Paranormals:

Sevyn

Smoke

The Box

Kindle Vella:

Love Lied Series

Audiobooks:

Connect on Social Media

Subscribe to my Newsletter or Paranormal Newsletter for exclusive updates on new releases, sneak peeks, and much more.

You can also follow me on:

Newsletter Sign up: https://mailchi.mp/c5ed185fd868/httpsmailchimp

Paranormal Newsletter Sign up: https://mailchi.mp/38b87cb6232d/keta-kendric-paranormal-newsletter

Instagram: https://instagram.com/ketakendric

Facebook Readers' Group: https://www.face-book.com/groups/380642765697205/

BookBub: https://www.bookbub.com/authors/keta-kendric

Twitter: https://twitter.com/AuthorKetaK

Goodreads: https://www.goodreads.com/user/show/73387641-keta-kendric

TikTok: https://www.tiktok.com/@ketakendric?

Pinterest: https://www.pinterest.com/authorslist/